SPLURCH ACADEMY

FOR DISRUPTIVE BOYS

THE TROUBLE WITH SQUIDS

GROSSET & DUNLAP
Published by the Penguin Group
Penguin Group (USA) Inc., 375 Hudson Street,
New York, New York 10014, USA
Penguin Group (Canada), 90 Eglinton Avenue East, Suite 700,
Toronto, Ontario M4P 2Y3, Canada
(a division of Pearson Penguin Canada Inc.)
Penguin Books Ltd., 80 Strand, London WC2R 0RL, England
Penguin Group Ireland, 25 St. Stephen's Green, Dublin 2, Ireland
(a division of Penguin Books Ltd.)
Penguin Group (Australia), 250 Camberwell Road, Camberwell,
Victoria 3124, Australia
(a division of Pearson Australia Group Pty. Ltd.)
Penguin Books India Pvt. Ltd., 11 Community Centre,
Panchsheel Park, New Delhi—110 017, India
Penguin Group (NZ), 67 Apollo Drive, Rosedale,
Auckland 0632, New Zealand
(a division of Pearson New Zealand Ltd.)
Penguin Books (South Africa) (Pty.) Ltd., 24 Sturdee Avenue,
Rosebank, Johannesburg 2196, South Africa

Penguin Books Ltd., Registered Offices:
80 Strand, London WC2R 0RL, England

Typeset in Imprint.

Library of Congress Control Number: 2010048678

ISBN 978-0-448-45362-0   10 9 8 7 6 5 4 3 2 1

SPLURCH ACADEMY

FOR DISRUPTIVE BOYS

THE
TROUBLE WITH
SQUIDS

by Julie Gardner Berry and Sally Faye Gardner

Grosset & Dunlap
An Imprint of Penguin Group (USA) Inc.

To our sister Jane,
who could never resist a critter.
—**J.G.B.** & **S.F.G.**

A Word of Warning
to All Disruptive Boys

If my past warnings haven't made you steer
clear of Splurch Academy, what can I say
here that will make a difference? By now
you know the sorry truth. You know that no
boy unlucky enough to be sent to Splurch
Academy ever returns. You know that the
teachers are monsters, and the headmaster,
Dr. Archibald Farley, is the worst of the
bunch—a cruel and conniving vampire. You
know that Dr. Farley will stop at nothing to
gain final control over the boys, once and for
all. He'll suck their brains out their ear canals
and swap them with the brains of trained rats.
He'll summon evil Egyptian gods to grant him
cosmic power over the boys. He'll even use
the powdered bones of his own dead relatives
to resurrect long-dead monsters, in hopes
that the monsters will eat the boys and rid
Farley of their pesky presence.

This is the kind of deranged personality
Cody Mack and his fifth-grade friends are
up against. I'd say their odds are pretty
pathetic, wouldn't you?

One of these days Dr. Farley and his creepy crew are bound to win and destroy Cody and his friends forever. It's not a matter of *if*, but *when*. Maybe it'll happen in the very book you're holding.

Don't blame me when you start having nightmares. Go ahead and tell yourself, "It's only a book. It isn't real. There's no such place as Splurch Academy."

We all have our little delusions.

If yours help you sleep at night, I won't try to talk you out of them.

I will tell you this, though.

I've got a bad feeling about this particular episode of Cody Mack's adventures. Something's not right. There's a foul stench in the air at Splurch Academy. Something fishy is brewing in Archibald Farley's evil laboratory. Hideous creatures lurk in underground channels, seething in the bubbling murk beneath the building's foundations. Cody and his friends are up a creek without a paddle. This story will *not* go well for them.

And I expect you still plan on reading all about it, don't you?

Well then, dive in.

Grade Five

Possibly the most disruptive bunch of boys Splurch Academy has ever seen.

Cody Mack, age 11

The Master of Disruption. The Sultan of Schemes. The Prince of Plots. The Demigod of Dastardly Deeds. A pint-size Lord of Chaos. The ringleader of the fifth-grade band of brothers, and every teacher's worst nightmare.

Carlos Ferrari, age 10

Cody Mack's best friend. Give him a rubber band, a paper clip, and a can of shaving cream, and he'll turn them into a weapon of mass *disruption*. It's not his fault things tend to blow up when he's around.

Mugsy, aka Percival Porsein, age 11

This kid will eat *anything* as long as it has ketchup on it. Don't tease him about his teddy bear or he'll sit on you. He has a habit of accidentally breaking things, like other people's ribs, but really, he means well.

Ratface, aka Rufus Larsen, age 10

The one kid at Splurch Academy who felt perfectly at home in a rat's body. He's whiny; he's annoying; he has weird ideas. Nothing is safe from this light-fingered little thief.

Sully, aka Sullivan Sanders, age 10

Brave as an earthworm. Athletic as cooked spaghetti. Minus his glasses he's as blind as a mole. Still, being a genius has its advantages. This bookworm won't speak to adults. Period.

Victor Schmitz, age 11

Anger issues got him sent to Splurch, and nothing's changed so far. A good pick for a tug-of-war team, but you don't want to challenge him to an arm-wrestling match. If you do, it's safer if *you* lose.

The Teachers

Dr. Archibald Farley, Headmaster

The egotistical mastermind behind the torture of innocent disruptive boys. With his vampire strength and his mad science cunning, this evil headmaster is never without a plan to make Cody and his friends suffer.

Nurse Bilgewater

Strong as an ox and as kind-hearted as a feeding shark, Beulah Bilgewater is Splurch Academy's medical specialist. Whatever you do, don't get sick. Once this evil nurse gets her tentacles on you, there's no escape.

Mr. Fronk

A lumbering carcass of a fifth-grade teacher who sleeps like a corpse through every class. His two fears: fire and boys who prefer comic books.

Griselda, the Cafeteria Lady

The only thing worse than her cooking is her complaining about her aches and pains. Wait. Never mind. Her cooking's worse.

Mr. Howell

Go ahead. Try to run away from Splurch Academy. This mangy fleabag will even give you a head start. He sprints like a wolf and gnaws on bones for lunch. Better steer clear when the moon comes out . . .

Ivanov, the Hall Monitor

This jack-of-all-trades does the dirty work of keeping the Academy clean. Sort of. He'd rather do the dirty work of tattling on kids.

Librarian

Does she have a name? Does she ever speak? Whose side is she on? No one is sure. But don't raise your voice in her library. Not if you want to own your own tongue.

Miss Threadbare

This bony, spindly, scraggly bag o' knuckles and teeth is Headmaster Farley's secretary by day—a bat-winged hawk-monster by night. Don't be slow when *she* tells you to stand for the pledge.

CHAPTER ONE
THE CHANDELIER

"Why are we doing this again?" Mugsy moaned, wrapping his arms and legs tightly around a chandelier post. "I hate heights!"

"Quiet!" Carlos warned. His hair was full of spiderwebs, and his hands were full of wires. "Just another minute, and we'll be done."

They were stringing wire round and round the iron frame of the massive chandelier that hung in the teachers' lounge. It had been so long since anyone dusted it that sheets of cobwebs draped across each metal spoke.

HURRY UP, GUYS. IF THEY CATCH US, FARLEY'LL PEEL US OPEN LIKE GRAPEFRUITS.

I TOLD YOU. THEY'RE ALL IN A STAFF MEETING DOWN IN FARLEY'S OFFICE. WE'VE GOT LOTS OF TIME.

From outside the Academy building they heard the rumble and roar of an engine. They turned to watch through the tall windows as Priscilla Prim's biplane sailed off into the sunset, carrying with it her five girl students. The girls lived at Splurch Academy now, but were off to celebrate the winter holidays in Greece on the shore of the sunny Mediterranean Sea. While the boys stayed stuck at Splurch Academy, the girls were exploring ancient ruins and searching for archaeological treasures. Nothing at Splurch was fair.

"Good riddance to stupid girls," Victor grumbled. "I don't care a bit that they're gone."

"Yeah," Ratface said. "Spending their vacation at the beach, building sand castles . . . who cares?"

"Even getting a vacation, period," Carlos said. "Nope. I'm not jealous."

"You're all pathetic liars, you know that?" Sully said.

"Keep still and stand guard!" Carlos ordered.

"Remind me again why we're doing this?" Mugsy asked. "I get a little woozy from extreme heights. Makes me forget stuff."

"How 'bout if you forget to whine all the time?" Victor snapped. "There. Am I doing it right, 'Los?"

Carlos nodded. "Perfect."

"Hey, quit swinging the lamp!" Mugsy wailed. "I'm getting seasick!"

"We're doing this, Mugsy," Cody explained, "because the faculty lounge chandelier is just the right size and made of the right stuff for Carlos to turn it into a satellite communicator. Once he's done, we can send a message to our parents and tell them what it's really like here. Once they know how we've suffered, they'll come rescue us!"

Ratface fed a length of wire to Victor. "Send them a message? How?"

"His communicator thingy sends the message by bouncing it off the moon," Victor said. "Or something."

"Off the satellites orbiting the earth through space," Carlos corrected.

4

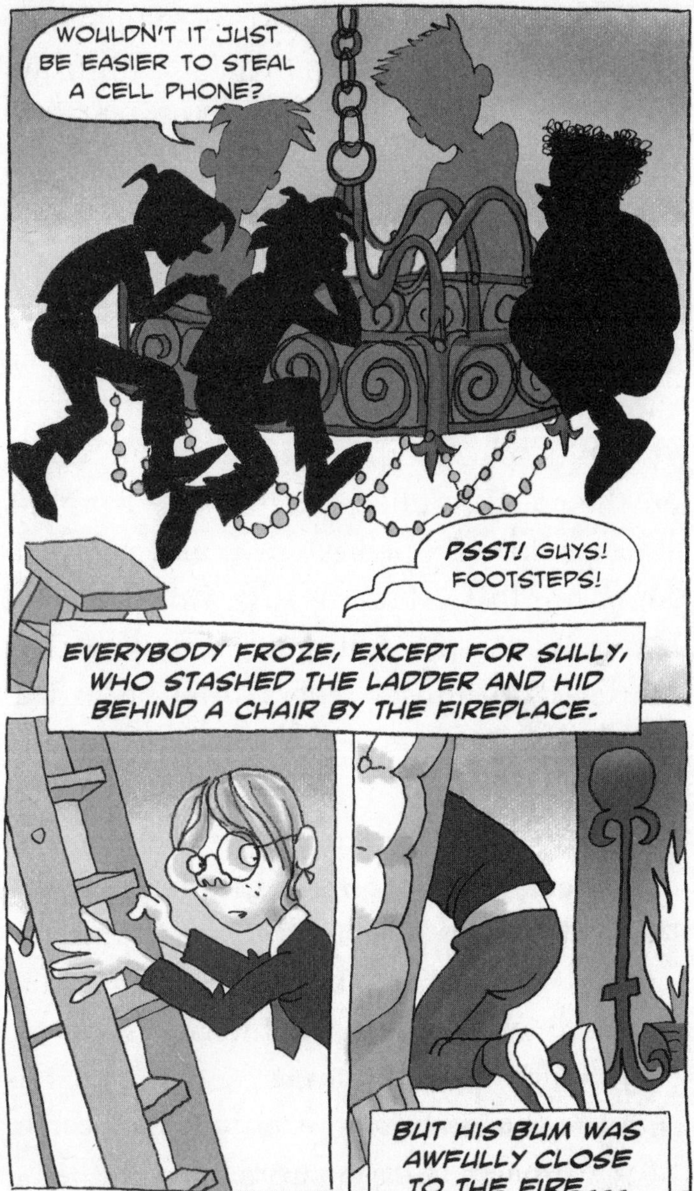
WOULDN'T IT JUST BE EASIER TO STEAL A CELL PHONE?
PSST! GUYS! FOOTSTEPS!
EVERYBODY FROZE, EXCEPT FOR SULLY, WHO STASHED THE LADDER AND HID BEHIND A CHAIR BY THE FIREPLACE.
BUT HIS BUM WAS AWFULLY CLOSE TO THE FIRE . . .

The door opened, and in came Mr. Fronk, the fifth-grade teacher and reanimated corpse. He peered this way and that, behind the door, being supersneaky. Cody held his breath. If he wanted to, Mr. Fronk could rip the boys' arms out of their sockets without even breaking a sweat. Fortunately it never occurred to their homeroom teacher that he should look *up*.

Fronk closed the door, flopped down on the couch, pulled a cell phone from his shirt pocket, flipped it open, and punched some numbers. His massive fingers could barely hit the tiny buttons correctly, and he muttered to himself every time he had to start over. Finally he succeeded in dialing and held the tiny phone up to his ear.

In the stillness of the room, Cody could hear the faraway ringing of the phone. Fronk leaned back, his face pointing up toward the ceiling. The boys in the chandelier gazed at one another with panic in their eyes.

But Mr. Fronk didn't see them. His thoughts were elsewhere.

A woman's voice answered the phone.

"Each minute that I sit trapped in a classroom of sauerkraut-brained boys only makes me long for you more, my lovely little buttered artichoke."

From behind the couch, Sully shifted slightly. *He must be getting toasty, so close to the fire*, Cody thought.

The door opened, and Cody sucked in his breath. Fronk snapped his cell phone shut and dropped it into his shirt pocket.

It was Headmaster Archibald Farley at the door, glaring at Fronk from underneath his bushy eyebrows. He carried a bucket of water, which he set down at his feet.

"There you are, Prometheus," he said.

"Er . . . yes," Fronk said. He wiped sweat off his brow. "I just, um, came in here to rest for a moment."

"You missed a good deal of our faculty meeting. I was waiting to tell you all about my latest research," Farley said.

Fronk looked guilty. He tried to change the subject. "What's the water for?"

Farley shrugged. "Just something I need to prepare for my experiment."

A movement caught Cody's eye. From up in the chandelier, Ratface pulled a bit of wire from his pocket and twisted it into a hook. He threaded a long string through the hook. Ratface, an accomplished thief, always had pockets full of this and that. Slowly, Ratface lowered his improvised fishing line down over Fronk's head.

Cody could only hope Farley wouldn't notice the dangling fishhook.

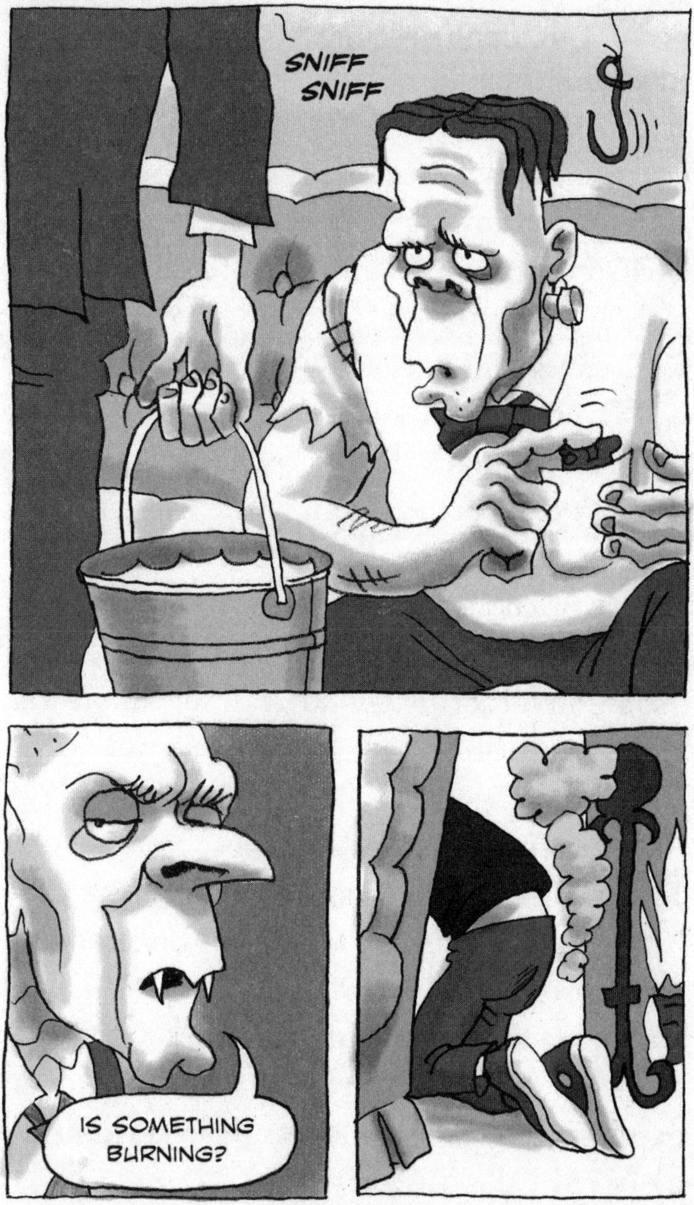
SNIFF
SNIFF
IS SOMETHING BURNING?

"While you were *resting*," Farley was saying, "the other faculty members drew straws to see which of them would be lucky enough to test my new procedure first. And can you believe it? You won the drawing."

Fronk frowned. "Oh, I can believe it, all right," he muttered.

Lower, lower went Ratface's fishhook.

"Everything I need for my experiment will be in place tomorrow," Farley went on. "The procedure won't take more than a moment. Just nip down to my laboratory before breakfast. It's completely painless."

"Now see here," Fronk protested. "My job description doesn't say anything about this kind of stuff. I'm not your guinea pig."

The fishhook was inches away from Fronk's shoulder. It swayed slightly. Cody held his breath. He was sure it was going to hook Fronk on the earlobe.

"Why me?" Fronk continued. "Why test your experiment on a teacher? Why not experiment on the kids and leave me out of it?"

Cody and the other boys exchanged nervous glances. Experimenting on the kids was an all-too-familiar strategy on the part of Dr. Archibald Farley, mad scientist and psychopath.

"You're already a monster," Dr. Farley said. "If anything goes wrong, no harm done. I get only one chance with the lads. I have to be sure of success."

"What do you *mean*, if anything goes wrong?" Fronk demanded. "I insist on knowing the risks beforehand." Then he stopped and sniffed the air. By now the smell of smoke was unmistakable.

"Of course, if you really don't want to assist in my research . . ." Farley inspected his fingernails. "There's a new position open here at Splurch. Perhaps I'll transfer you into it. Dorm Mom to the fifth-grade boys."

"What?" Fronk yelped. "You can't!"

"You get to put bandages on their boo-boos, read them stories, and tuck them in at night. It pays half of what a teacher makes, but money isn't everything."

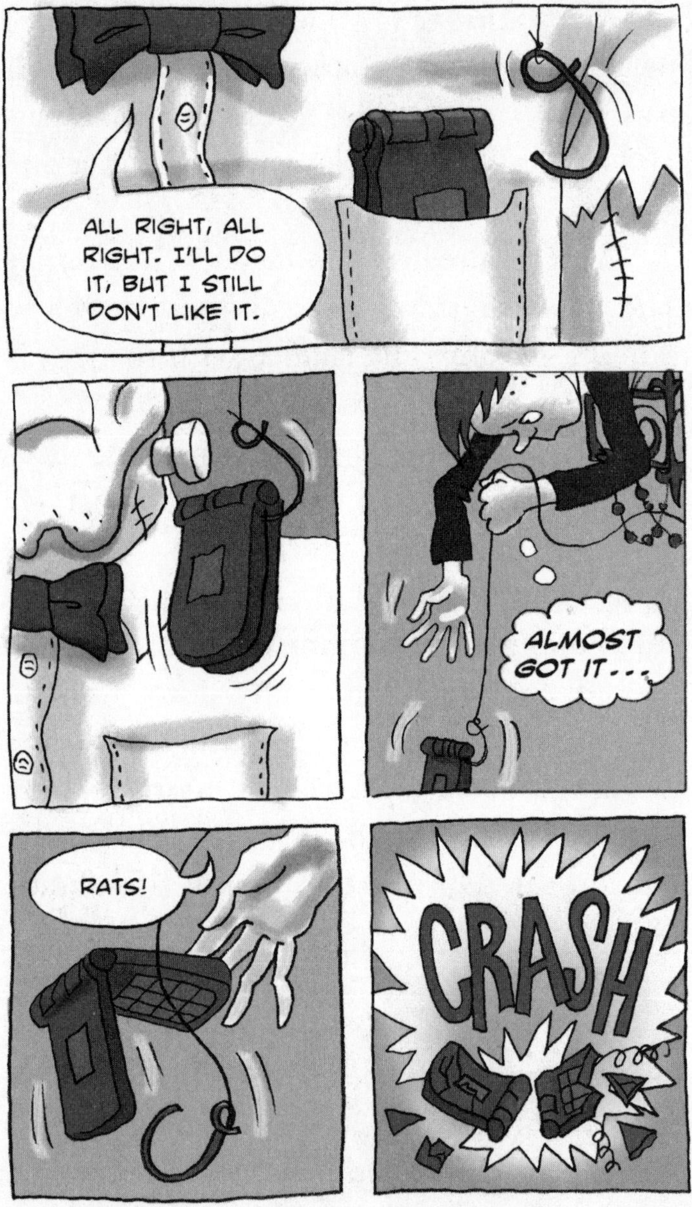
ALL RIGHT, ALL RIGHT. I'LL DO IT, BUT I STILL DON'T LIKE IT.
ALMOST GOT IT . . .
RATS!
CRASH

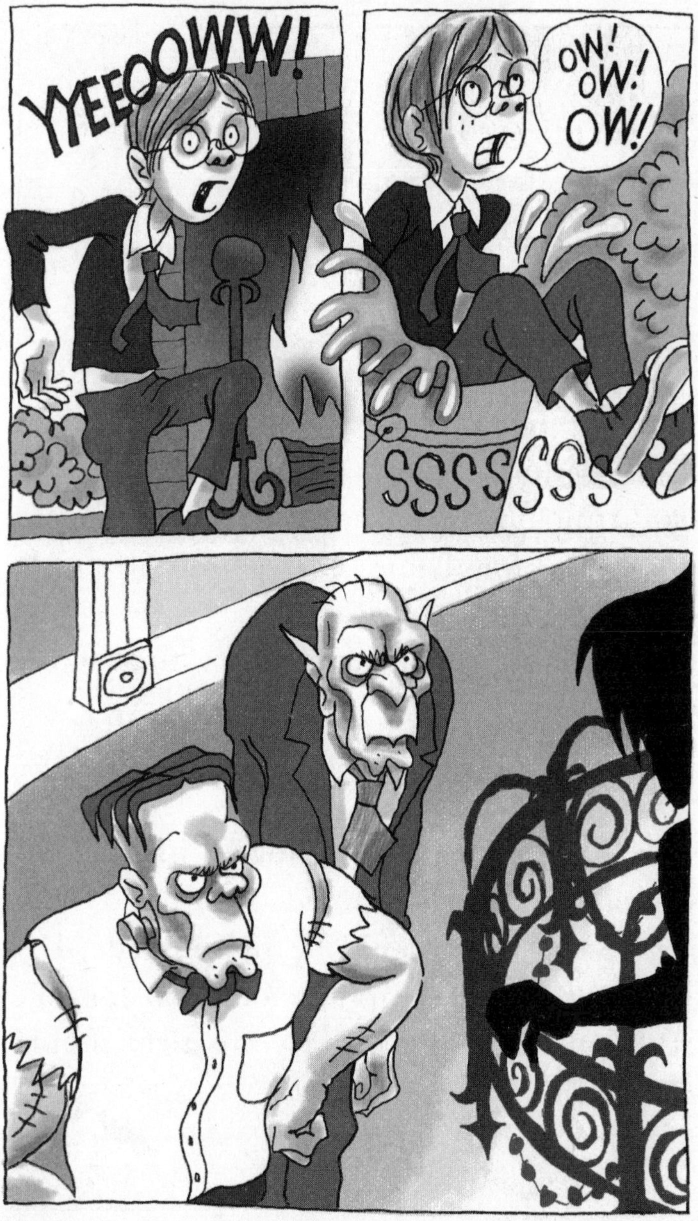
YYEEOOWW!
OW! OW! OW!
SSSSSSSs

"The fifth grade," Farley observed. "Always the fifth grade. This is your class, Prometheus. I expect you to keep them under better control."

Fronk gathered up the boys in his huge, stitched-on arms. "Come on, vermin. It's off to detention for you."

"Just don't forget our little appointment in the laboratory, Prometheus," Farley said. "Sunrise. Don't be late." He handed a squirming Sully to the Frankenteacher.

"Fronk and his girlfriend, sitting in a tree," Cody sang as loud as he could. "K-i-s-s-i-n-g. First comes love, then comes marriage—"

Fronk's face flushed puce with rage. "Stuff it, you twerp!"

"Then comes a zombie in a baby carriage!" Cody screamed.

"Shut your mouth!" Fronk hissed. "I've had enough. Detention's too good for you. I know what'll clean up your dirty minds. Right this way, boys."

CHAPTER TWO

THE VISITOR

"Detention in chains would have been better than this," Victor said. He chiseled hard, stinky gunk off a tile floor.

"I don't know," Ratface said, making a face. "I actually enjoy being made to clean the faculty men's bathroom with my bare hands. It's refreshing."

"How long would you say it's been since this bathroom's been scrubbed, Cody?" Carlos asked. He dumped more scrubbing powder in the sink.

"A thousand years," Cody said. "Give or take."

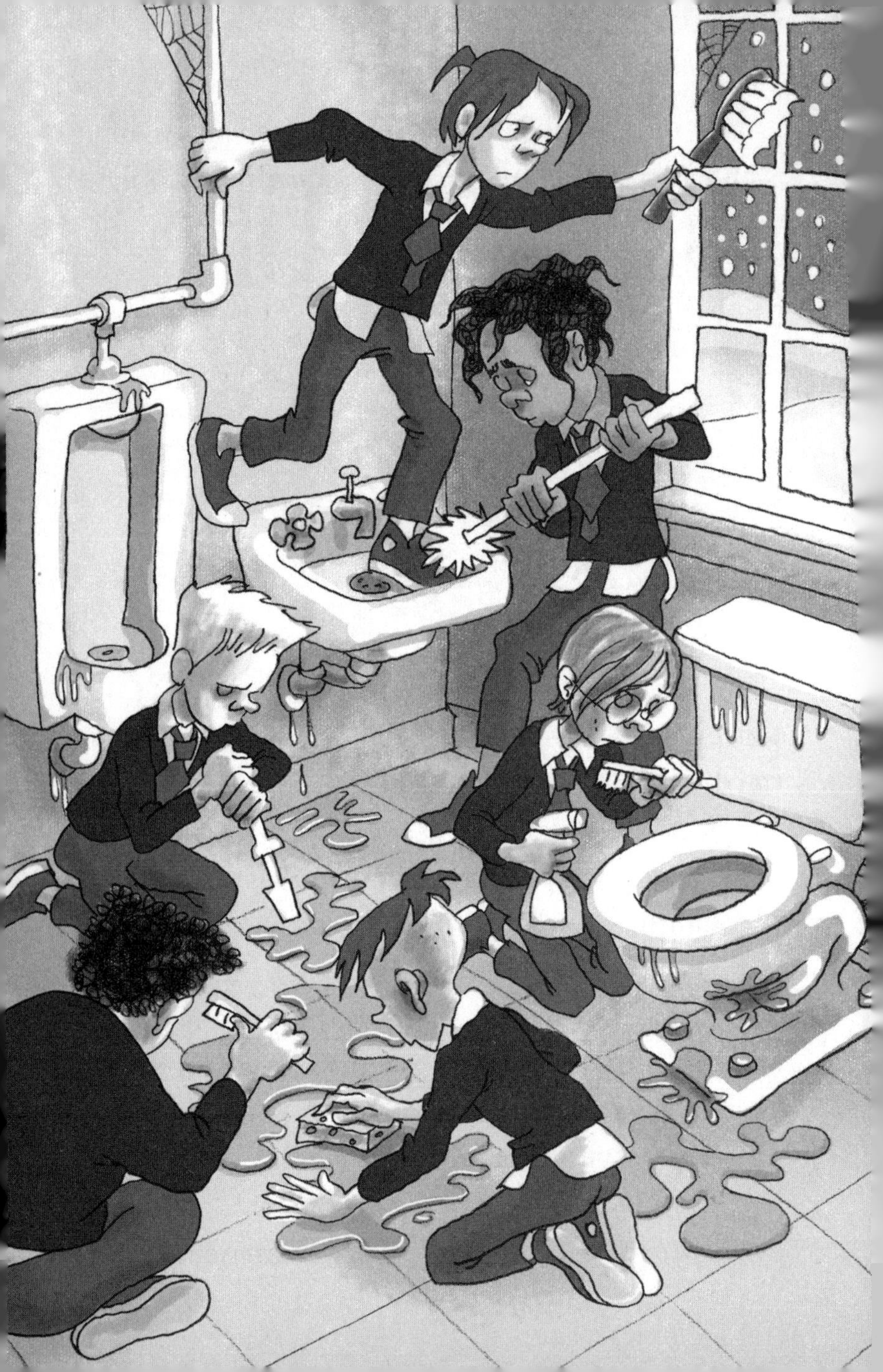

"I don't know about you guys," Mugsy said, "but after this, I'll never be able to look the same way at a urinal again."

"They should use this room as a biology classroom," Sully said. "It's got its own ecosystem. Bacterial colonies, nests of bugs, families of frogs living in the drains . . . it's educational, really."

"Must be a monster thing." Ratface wrinkled his nose. "I've never smelled a bathroom like *this* before."

"Hey, look, everybody," Mugsy said. "It's snowing!"

They looked out the window. Sure enough, fat white flakes were spiraling down from the night sky outside. Thicker and faster they came. The wind picked up, blowing the snow around in driving sheets. The night seemed gray instead of black.

"A blizzard," Victor said. "Back home I would've been all excited. It would mean a snow day tomorrow. No school!"

"No such thing as a snow day here, I bet," Ratface said.

"Someone's coming," Cody whispered.

They switched off the bathroom lights and peeked out the doorway.

Miss Threadbare, the secretary, and Mr. Howell, a teacher, came into view. Miss Threadbare pulled back one of the drapes from a ground-level window.

THE STORM'S A BAD ONE.

I DON'T MIND THE SNOW.

ARCHIE DOES. HE'S LIKELY TO CANCEL TONIGHT'S HUNT.

A TOMB IS COLD, ISN'T IT? HE SPOILS ALL OUR FUN.

"Cold makes his arthritis flare up in his knees. He's more interested in his research right now, anyway," Threadbare pointed out. "He keeps saying he's really onto something this time. Except there's some missing ingredient he's waiting for, and he won't say what it is or when it will get here."

"Experiments schmeriments," Howell growled. "Farley's always making things complicated. We want to get rid of the boys? I say we do it the old-fashioned way. Eat 'em. Nothing elaborate, just a little salt and pepper . . ."

"I'm partial to Tabasco sauce, myself," Threadbare said. "Or roasted on a spit with a nice lemon butter sauce." She sighed. "But you know what happened last time Farley tried to hurt the boys, Howell. Major trouble. We can't eat them. We can't even hurt them." She smiled, showing her nasty teeth. "But there's nothing saying we can't *change* them."

"Fine, fine" Howell said. "Farley can experiment on the boys all he wants. But he'd better keep his mitts off me."

Howell looked out the window once more and growled low in his throat. "I hate nights where we can't go hunting. So boring. If we can't go out tonight, I'm gonna go watch *Thriller* on BooTube."

And together they walked away.

"Did you hear that?" Cody said when the teachers were out of hearing.

"Yeah," Victor said. "Farley's cooking up a new way to mess with our heads. I am *not* letting him suck my brain out again."

"No, not that," Cody said. "The hunt is canceled tonight. Do you realize what that means? It means if we can somehow get outside, we can get free! There'll be no one outside to see us or stop us. We can make a run for it!"

"Maybe on our way," Mugsy said, "we can stop at a burger place for some fries with ketchup."

"Let me point out a few wrinkles in your plan," Sully said. "One: It's forty below outside and blizzarding. Two: We have no coats, boots, mittens, or gloves. We'd get lost in the snow and freeze to death in less than an hour. Three: Once they notice we're gone, they'll come after us. Howell, the wolf-man, will have no trouble following our tracks."

Cody bit his lip and said nothing. Sully was right and he knew it, but that didn't mean he had to like it. There must be some way . . .

The silence was broken by the sound of a clanging gong going off. It hung on the wall near the bathroom door so the noise nearly deafened the boys.

"It's a doorbell," Victor whispered. "Who'd be coming here this late at night?"

"And in a storm?" Carlos added.

They watched and waited. Ivanov, the hunchbacked hall monitor, shuffled into view with Pavlov, the Hound of Death, trotting at his heels. Pavlov looked at the boys, bared his teeth, and growled.

"Hush, boy," Ivanov scolded. "That's no way to greet our visitors."

He pulled the door open. In a flurry of swirling snow, someone stepped inside.

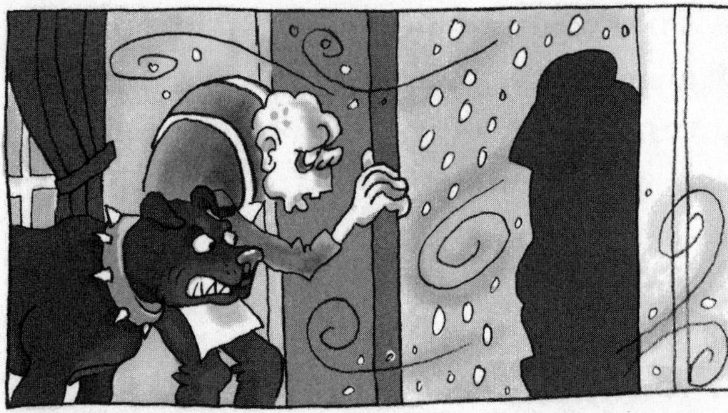

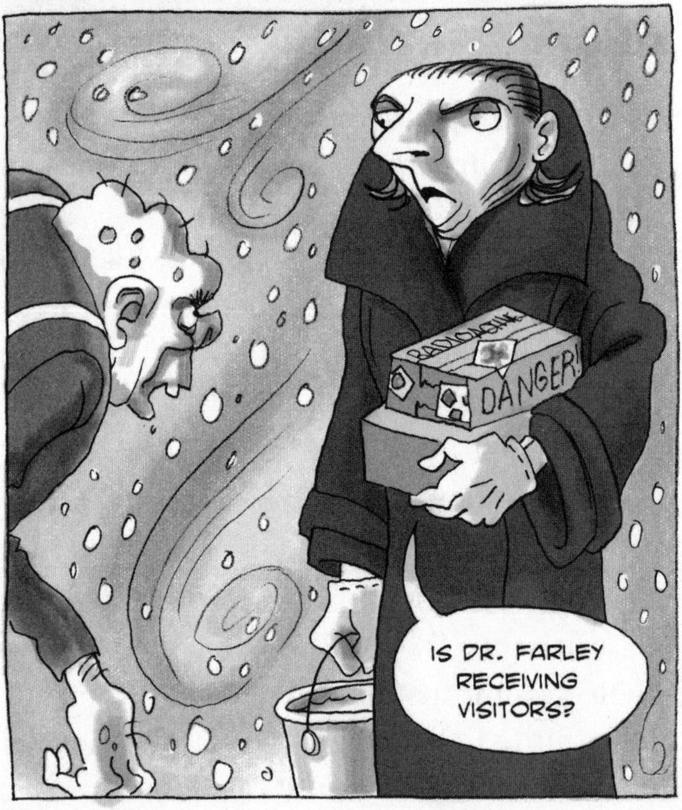
DANGER!
IS DR. FARLEY RECEIVING VISITORS?

Her voice was soft, feathery soft, yet strange. Cody strained to listen. She stared at Ivanov with an unblinking gaze that made him take a step back.

"I—I'll check," Ivanov stuttered. He turned and hobbled as fast as his crippled legs would take him down the corridor.

Farley soon appeared. He bared his fangs in his most welcoming hideous smile.

"Professor Eelpot," he said, bowing low. "Welcome to Splurch Academy. How very good of you to join us."

Cody's jaw dropped. *Professor* Eelpot? *Join* us? Oh no! Not another freaky monster teacher.

"The pleasure is all mine, Archibald" Professor Eelpot's soft voice said. "Now that we have finally reached an agreement on my salary."

"Yes. Well, I would rather you not mention your salary to the other faculty." He caughed. "At any rate, I've had the science room dusted and prepared for your arrival." He held out his hand. "And now, if I may . . . ?"

MAY I HELP YOU WITH YOUR PAIL?

NO.

THAT... IS MY PET.

THE SUPPLIES YOU ASKED ME TO BRING ARE IN HERE.

"It's so beautifully simple," Farley whispered. "I don't know why I never thought of it before."

"Because you never paid attention in science class like you should have," Professor Eelpot whispered eerily. "Knowledge is power, Archibald."

Farley patted her on the shoulder. "Well, now you're here," he said. "Won't you come inside and join me for a Bloody Harry?"

Professor Eelpot shrugged out of her jacket, revealing a stiff, white lab coat underneath. "Who's Harry?"

Farley grinned. "The mailman."

CHAPTER THREE
THE SPECIMEN

The next morning Cody shivered himself awake, only to see icicles hanging from the windows in their dormitory, which was nothing more than the old refurbished stables of Splurch Academy. The boys slept in horse stalls on piles of moldy straw with only one rat-chewed blanket apiece. They looked out the windows to see snow piled in eight-foot drifts around the building with more dumping down every second.

Carlos came into the room and knelt down by Cody.

HEY, LOOK WHAT I'VE GOT. I WENT BACK TO THE TEACHERS' LOUNGE THIS MORNING AND SCROUNGED UP ALL THE BROKEN PIECES TO FRONK'S CELL PHONE.

WHAT FOR?

Carlos stuffed all the pieces into his pockets. "There's lots of microtechnology in a cell phone," he explained. "I can use it to make my communicator device."

Ratface slept curled in a shivering ball, his teeth chattering. Cody kicked his feet. "Wake up, Ratface," he said. "You'll feel warmer if you move around."

One by one the other boys rose, stretched, and trudged to the cafeteria. They passed by Dr. Farley and Nurse Bilgewater in the midst of a whispered conversation. Cody perked up his ears. He could just make out what they were saying.

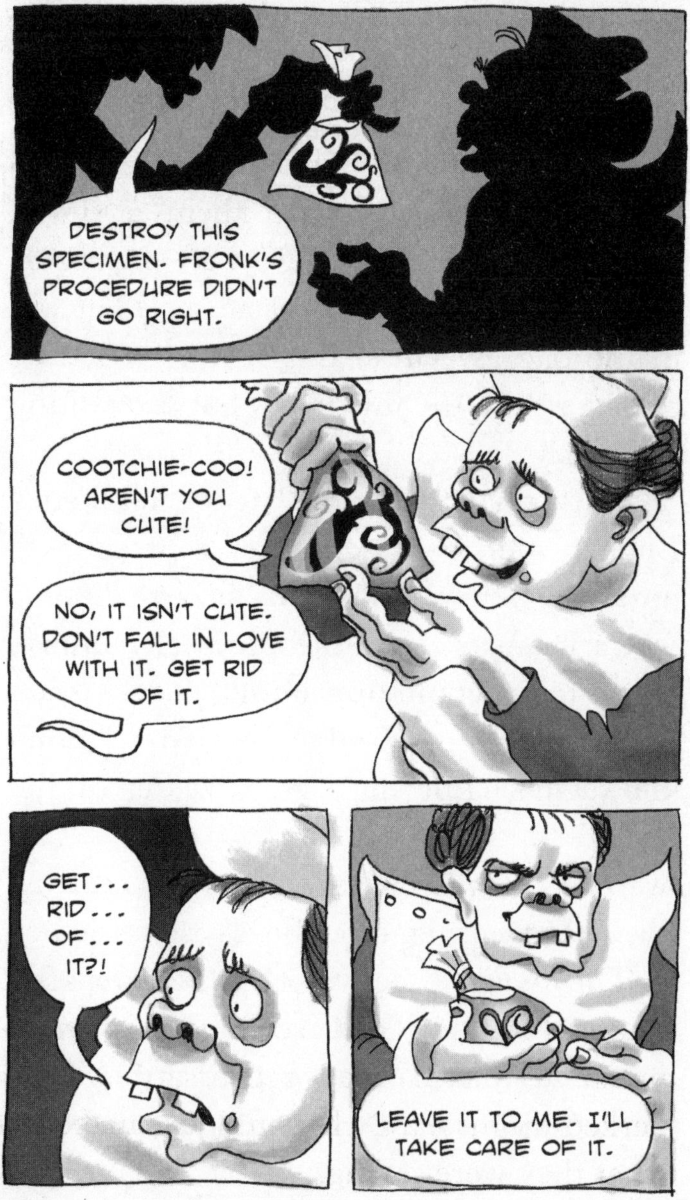
DESTROY THIS SPECIMEN. FRONK'S PROCEDURE DIDN'T GO RIGHT.
COOTCHIE-COO! AREN'T YOU CUTE!
NO, IT ISN'T CUTE. DON'T FALL IN LOVE WITH IT. GET RID OF IT.
GET... RID... OF... IT?!
LEAVE IT TO ME. I'LL TAKE CARE OF IT.

"I'm counting on you to get this done right," Farley told her. "I know how softhearted you are."

Victor and Ratface snorted with laughter, and Cody gave them a shove. "*Shhh!* Or they'll know we were spying on them." He craned his neck to see what was in the bag as Nurse Bilgewater passed by on her way to the infirmary, but he couldn't really tell.

Sully poked at his plate of blackened English muffin hockey pucks spread with horseradish jelly. "That was bizarre."

Carlos used the horseradish jelly squirty bottle to draw pictures on his plate. "She's up to something, Cody," he said. "I don't know what. But she's got a secret of her own."

"Let's go spy on her and figure out what it is," Ratface suggested.

They left their crummy breakfast untouched and tiptoed down the hall toward the nurse's office. They peered through the window to see what their hideous nurse was up to.

"I don't know about you," Victor said, "but dumping a bag of stuff into a fish tank and filling it up with shiny colored stones, a toy scuba diver, and a treasure chest hardly seems like 'getting rid of' something."

"She's not following Farley's orders," Mugsy concluded. "Wonder what he'll say when he finds out."

"For once it won't be us in trouble." Ratface giggled. A little too loudly.

Bilgewater stiffened and turned to see where the noise came from.

"Duck!" Ratface warned. "Here. Into this closet."

They could hear her heavy footsteps lumbering toward the door. Ratface held the closet door open while the boys all scooted through. Only it was not a closet. A narrow staircase wound through the dimly lit space behind the door.

Cody pulled the door shut as softly as he could.

"Hurry! Go up! Go up!" Cody whispered. "If she comes after us, we'll be trapped and cornered!"

They tiptoed up the stairs until the bottom floor was out of sight, then paused to listen for Bilgewater.

"We made it," Carlos said. "Wonder where these stairs go." They looked around at the narrow stairwell. It led up incredibly high to a landing with a ladder reaching up to a trapdoor.

"Looks like it must lead to the roof," Sully said.

"Excellent! Let's go." Ratface started climbing up.

"It's blizzarding out, remember?" Sully said. "We'll get blown off the roof."

"Phooey," Victor said. "Maybe the blizzard will blow us home. Don't be a wimp. Come on, let's see what's there. Up and out!"

They climbed up and up, story after story, spiraling round and round until Cody thought he might puke. The stairs creaked under their feet, and he wondered if one of the teachers would hear them. Sully panted with each step.

They reached the top. Victor opened the

trapdoor and pushed his way through onto the snow-covered roof. Sparkling gusts of snow swirled down onto their hair and noses. One by one they all climbed onto the roof.

"Awesome!" Ratface cried. "Wish I had a sled. I could slide right off this roof and land in those snowdrifts."

"Yeah, and break your neck," Carlos said.

"We'll die of pneumonia up here," Sully said, shivering.

"We're just here to take a look, Sully,"

Cody told him. "Five minutes won't kill us."

POW! Victor plastered the side of Sully's face with a snowball. Soon they were all going at it in a furious snowball war. Then the sound of a truck engine backing through the driveway made them stop.

"See anything down there?" Carlos said. "What's going on?"

"In all this snow, I can barely make it out," Cody said. "Someone's moving around down there. That might be Farley in the cape."

"Let's go. We'll be late for class." Sully shivered. "Mr. Fronk'll be furious."

"Are you kidding? He'll be fast asleep, napping," Cody said. "Guys, listen! I've got a plan. Let's slide off this roof and land on top of that truck. When it leaves, we'll go with it, and we're free!"

The boys all stared at him. Their noses were starting to turn blue.

"Free and dead, you mean," Sully said. "'Live free or die' is the state motto of New Hampshire, but it sure isn't mine."

"We won't die!" Cody cried. "The snow will cushion our fall!"

Carlos squinted through the swirling snow, trying to read the letters on the side of the truck. "Sid's Aquatic Supply," he read. "Serving Monsters and Mad Scientists since 1277."

"Yeah, um, Cody?" Victor said. "I don't think that truck's a good way for us to escape."

"Sully's turning blue," Mugsy said. "C'mon. Let's get to class."

CHAPTER FOUR
THE TENTACLE

The boys defrosted themselves and tiptoed into Mr. Fronk's classroom so as not to wake him from his nap. They found him, as usual, asleep behind his desk, his head leaning to one side, and his power cord plugged into the wall. But just as Cody slid into his chair, he heard the clicking sound of chalk on a chalkboard. He looked up.

Fronk was awake, shuffling papers on his desk. And a tentacled arm, poking out from behind his back, was writing on the chalkboard!

OPEN YOUR SPELLING BOOKS TO PAGE

"Whoa! Wait! Mr. Fronk!" Cody yelped.

His teacher fixed his yellow-eyed gaze on Cody. "Yes? What is it? What's so important that you must disturb my lesson?"

Behind him, the arm, thick and gross, kept on writing, listing out spelling words.

Cody could barely find the words to speak. Did Fronk know about this arm? How could he not? There it was, writing out his lessons.

Lessons?

"It's just . . . ," Cody said lamely. "It's just that, uh, you don't usually do spelling first. You do, um, math."

Carlos made a weird face at Cody.

"S-Sully," Carlos stuttered, "w-what's going on here?"

Sully shook his head, dumbfounded.

"He's . . . he's like a monster!" Ratface yelped.

"Duh, he already is a monster," Victor said. "What else is new?"

"Yeah, but we were used to that monster," Ratface said. "Now he's more monstery."

"Silence," Mr. Fronk's mouth said. "Anyone who speaks will be torn into bits, ground to a pulp, and devoured."

Fronk stopped, frowned, and shook his head. It seemed as if he was surprised by what he'd said. The ancient rules governing the Academy prohibited teachers from eating kids inside the building.

There was nothing else to do but pretend to do schoolwork. Cody dug inside his desk, found an old English textbook, and flipped through the pages. Borrrrrr-ing. The day went on like this forever until the classroom door opened, and Headmaster

Farley entered the room.

"How are you this morning, Fronk, old boy?" Dr. Farley asked brightly. He could clearly see Fronk's tentacles, but they didn't seem to surprise him.

Cody waited for Farley to explode, but he only smiled. "Excellent, excellent!" he said. He rubbed his hands together, then gestured to the boys.

"Come with me, lads," he said. "There's a change to your class schedule. You'll still spend most of your school day in here with Mr. Fronk. But starting today, you'll have a mid-morning science class period with our newest faculty member, Professor Eelpot. If you'd be so kind as to follow me?"

Cody hated it when Farley pretended to be all polite and gentlemanly. It was always an act and a crummy one at that.

The boys trooped down the hall after Farley. They turned a corner and saw a table that usually wasn't there. Pieces of candy were scattered across the table along with several different hats. It looked like someone was preparing for a costume party.

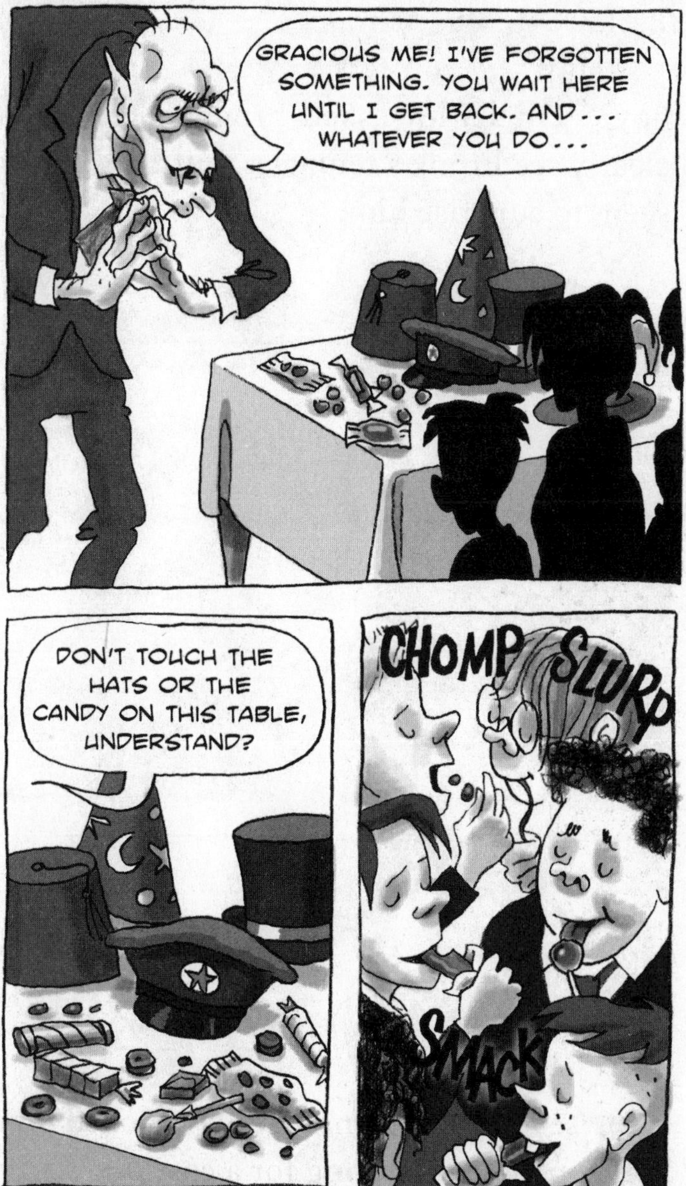
GRACIOUS ME! I'VE FORGOTTEN SOMETHING. YOU WAIT HERE UNTIL I GET BACK. AND... WHATEVER YOU DO...
DON'T TOUCH THE HATS OR THE CANDY ON THIS TABLE, UNDERSTAND?
CHOMP
SLURP
SMACK

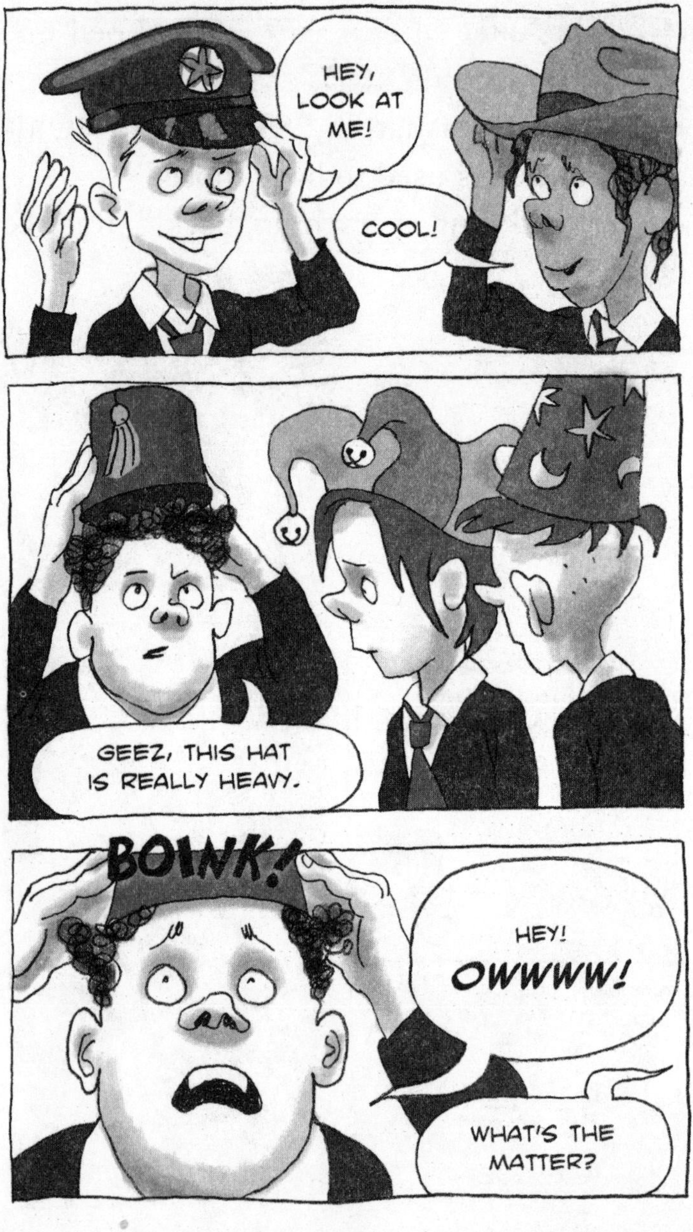
HEY, LOOK AT ME!
COOL!
GEEZ, THIS HAT IS REALLY HEAVY.
BOINK!
HEY! OWWWW!
WHAT'S THE MATTER?

"The hat!" Mugsy said. "It stabbed me. Something inside it was sharp."

"Probably a hatpin," Sully said. "Old-fashioned hats used to have those."

"Quick! Put everything back!" Ratface hissed. "Farley's coming!"

They threw the hats back on the table and tried to hide the candy wrappers. When Farley returned they were looking their most innocent.

Farley inspected the table and rubbed his hands together once more. "Well then," he said. "Time for science class. Professor Eelpot can't wait to eat you. Meet you, that is! A mere slip of the tongue. Ha-ha! Right this way, lads."

CHAPTER FIVE
THE TEACHER

Farley opened the door to the science lab. No one was there. A sign on the desk read MARLIN EELPOT, PHD.

The science lab was pretty cool. Carlos went straight for the electrical gadgets. Cody ignited a Bunsen burner and thought about the good old days, when he'd set Honey Bee Elementary on fire, back before he ever came to Splurch. Mugsy went straight for the walls where huge fish tanks stood stacked on top of one another like building blocks. Fluorescent light gleamed on the colored pebbles.

AWESOME!

WHAT'S THAT?

IT'S AN ELECTRIC EEL.

RULE NUMBER ONE...

NEVER TOUCH ETHEL, MY PET ELECTROPHORUS, UNLESS YOU WISH TO BE SIZZLED LIKE A SAUSAGE.

46

The boys backed away from the tank. One look at their new science teacher, and they sure weren't about to mess with Ethel.

The new teacher wore a white lab coat and clasped her hands behind her back. Her black-rimmed eyes seemed to bulge out of her head and stare at each boy, regardless of where they were in the room. They shuddered. She did not smile.

"Thank you, Dr. Farley," Professor Eelpot whispered. "You may go now. I will take over from here."

Farley raised a finger and opened his mouth to protest—Cody knew he wasn't used to taking orders from his staff—but then he seemed to change his mind. He left.

Professor Eelpot paced the front of the room, her hands still clasped tightly behind her back.

"Take a seat," she purred. Cody and the other boys sat down.

"Welcome to science class," she said. "In this room you will learn the mysteries of the natural world like you've never learned them before."

Cody had a feeling she was right about that—and he wasn't altogether sure this was a good thing.

"Now raise your hand if you think you know," she went on, "what we will study in science class."

Carlos's hand shot up in the air. "Galileo?" he cried. "Copernicus? Isaac Newton? Charles Darwin? Louis Pasteur? Albert Einstein? Stephen Hawking?"

"Geez, Carlos," Ratface muttered. "You're making the rest of us look stupid."

"Like that's hard," Victor snorted.

"I know you are, but what am I?" Ratface snapped.

Professor Eelpot ignored Victor and Ratface. "What is your name?" she asked.

"Carlos."

"Very well, Carlos. Do you know what all those men had in common?"

Carlos's Adam's apple bobbed up and down. He seemed suddenly less confident. "They were all groundbreaking scientists, er, ma'am?"

Professor Eelpot leaned closer to Carlos.

She shook her head and showed her pointy teeth. "No," she said. "They were all imbeciles."

Sully flinched as if someone had just punched him. Carlos's jaw dropped open.

Professor Eelpot pointed at a huge ocean mural on the wall. On it were terrifying pictures of hideous sea creatures with razor-sharp fangs and massive jaws.

"Long before your petty scientists appeared, long before insignificant mankind crawled out from its puddle, millions of years before dinosaurs tottered around on dry mud, mighty creatures ruled the seas," she said, still in her creepy whisper. Her eyes bulged like golf balls. "The mightiest of all the sea creatures—the one that has survived through the years and still dominates the seas—does anyone know what that is?"

Mugsy raised a quavering hand. "Um . . . the killer whale?"

Professor Eelpot turned her stare on him. "No, you dim-witted sea urchin," she purred. "I am not talking about pathetic whales."

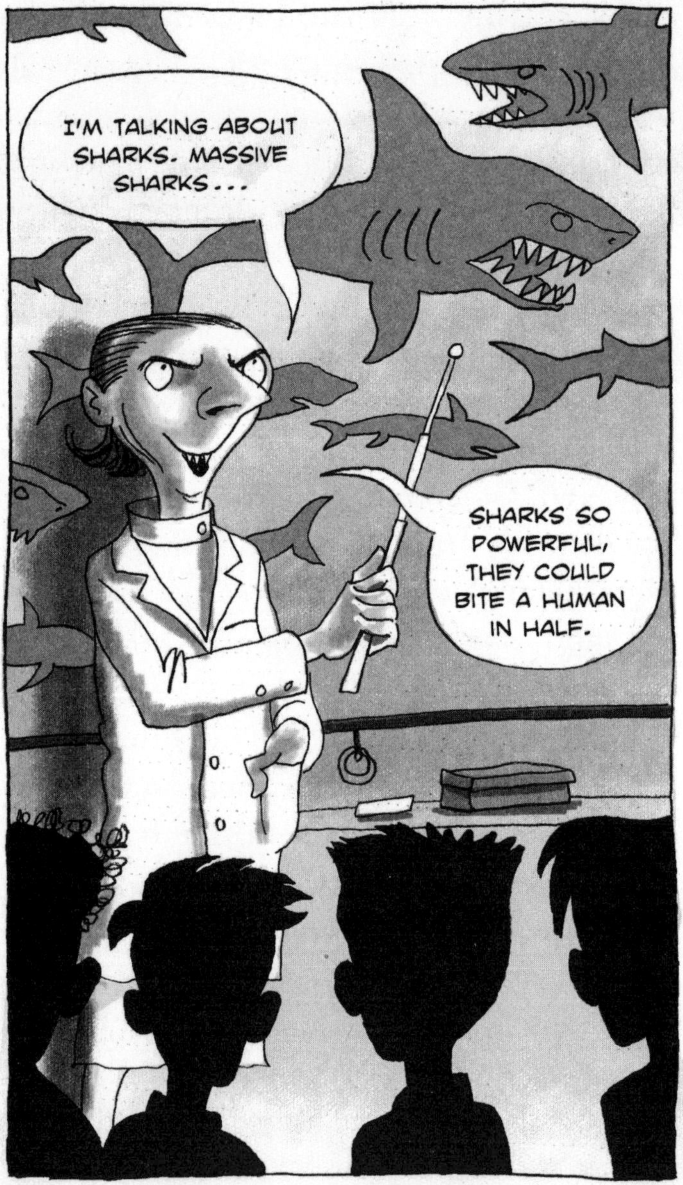
I'M TALKING ABOUT SHARKS. MASSIVE SHARKS . . .
SHARKS SO POWERFUL, THEY COULD BITE A HUMAN IN HALF.

She snapped her jaws. Then she whacked the tip of her pointer on the mural. "Here's the mighty great white. Here's the handsome hammerhead. And here." She pointed to a picture of a truly gigantic shark. "This big beauty, the Megalodon, is the largest shark that ever lived and one of the largest fish that ever existed. It could grow to be sixty-seven or more feet long. Its jaws were large enough to devour whales." She paused and shivered with delight. "What a *delicious* thought. Those arrogant mammals, honking and bobbing to the surface like corks . . ."

The boys stared at her.

"This feisty shark, the Cretoxyrhina, wasn't quite as large as the Megalodon, but it was much larger than today's great whites, at twenty-five feet or more in length. It's nicknamed the Ginsu shark, just like the famous kitchen knives, for how it *slices* and *dices* its prey. It shredded great tuna and swordfish and sailfish into juicy, tangy, bloody strips and gobbled them down. *Ahh!*" She sighed and licked her lips.

Professor Eelpot opened a drawer and pulled out a set of Ginsu knives. Then she opened a rubber tub full of foul-smelling somethings. The stink made Cody want to gag. "We're going to do some slicing and dicing of our own today to learn more about life in the sea, starting toward the bottom of the food chain." She gestured toward Ratface. "You. Come up here."

Ratface trotted to the front of the room.

"You've chosen a sea slug," Professor Eelpot whispered. "They go so beautifully with garlic sauce. You'll enjoy cutting him open and ripping his guts out."

Ratface's eyes rolled back in his head. He staggered back to his seat.

"Next?" Professor Eelpot said.

Mugsy came forward and also pulled a sea slug from the nasty pot. He sniffed it over and over the way a dog sniffs a dead squirrel before eating it.

Professor Eelpot licked her lips. "You have good taste, young man," she said. "Sea slugs go so nicely in a casserole," she said. "Next?"

When it came time for Sully's turn, Cody got a disgusting sea creature for him. Cody knew Sully wouldn't speak aloud in front of Professor Eelpot, but he was pretty sure his brainiac friend would much rather read about sea creatures than chop them open.

He poked at his own sea anemone. Cody Mack wasn't afraid of much, but he felt he'd really rather not do this. Not today, anyway.

"This is how you begin," Professor Eelpot began,

slicing a long gash through her sea worm with a knife. "Mmmm. I got a plump, juicy one."

Yuck!

The lunch bell rang. Saved by the bell!

Professor Eelpot's mouth curved down into a frown. "Seal your specimens in these plastic bags and wash up," she said. "We'll resume our dissection tomorrow." And with that, she disappeared into her office adjoining the classroom and shut the door.

Gagging and pinching their noses, the boys put away their sea creatures, then washed the nasty formaldehyde chemical smell off their hands.

"Ordinarily I don't believe in washing up before lunch," Ratface declared, "but those

I'LL BET THESE WOULD BE PRETTY GOOD WITH SOME TERIYAKI SAUCE...

WHAT'S COME OVER YOU, MUGS?

sea slime things are vile. *Blech!*"

Mugsy only shrugged.

"We've got to get out of this prison," Victor said. "It's scrambling all our heads."

Carlos rinsed a mountain of soap bubbles off his hands and watched it swirl down the drain. "Water is the only thing that knows how to get out of this place," he observed.

"What'd you just say, 'Los?" Sully asked.

"Oh, nothing. I said, water is the only thing that has a way out of Splurch Academy."

Cody and Sully looked at each other. Cody knew they were both thinking the same thing.

"Then that means," Cody said, "all we need to do to bust out is follow the water. If it can get out, so can we."

CHAPTER SIX
THE PIPES

Lunch was halfway normal food for once—hot dogs and tater tots. The hot dogs looked sort of green, but when Cody covered them with enough ketchup, he hardly noticed.

"Your lucky day, huh, Mugs?" Cody said. "Here's the ketchup for you. I know you'll probably want a whole bottle for yourself."

Mugsy wrinkled his nose. "Nah," he said. "I'm not in the mood for any of this stuff. Hey, look. Griselda's out in the hallway. Make sure she stays there. I'm going to go raid the pantry and see if there's something I like better."

"What's come over Mugsy?" Ratface said. "I can't believe he'd pass up ketchup!"

"Maybe he's sick," Carlos said.

"Did you notice how strange he was acting in science class?" Sully said.

Victor shivered. "The strange one in science class was that Eelpot lady. I didn't think anything at Splurch Academy could surprise me anymore, but she gives me the creeps."

Mugsy returned with his arms loaded down with cans and a can opener. "Look at this incredible stuff I got," he said. He cranked them open with his can opener, then dumped the contents right in his mouth. "Oysters," he said. "And salmon." *Gulp*. "And lots and lots of sardines!"

They all sat still as Farley passed slowly by their table. They pretended not to notice he was there. But Cody saw Farley's eyes pass over the lunch table and linger on Mugsy's cans of fish. A small smile passed his lips. Then he moved on, handing Nurse Bilgewater a bag full of water and some vague, squishy-looking thing inside.

"You know what to do," Dr. Farley said. Nurse Bilgewater nodded. Then when Farley was out of sight, she smiled, beaming at the contents of the bag like it held fluffy kitties. She hurried off to her infirmary.

"Oog, let's get out of here," Cody said. "I'm not hungry anymore."

They headed down the hall toward

their classroom, passing by the infirmary on the way. Sully tugged on Cody's sleeve and pointed. There was Nurse Bilgewater, opening a sewer valve in a large pipe that ran along the infirmary wall. She scooped something out of her aquarium with a lemonade pitcher and dumped it into the opening.

The boys ducked out of sight before she could look up and catch them spying on her. "What does it all mean?" Carlos asked.

"Who was she talking to?" Sully added.

Cody thumped his fist in his palm. "There's only one way to find out. C'mon. We have time. Let's take a quick trip down to the sewers and see if we can find out."

They checked both ways to make sure no teachers were watching them, then hurried down the cellar stairs to the sewer entry gate. They ducked through and made their way along the ledge that jutted out over the nasty sewer water.

But not Mugsy. He waded right through the sewer water, frolicking and splashing and making goofy, happy faces.

They hoisted him by the shoulders out of the water and dragged him along with them. But he kept trying to go back in. What was the matter with him? Cody was worried about his friend. But even if something was wrong, what could Cody do? He couldn't stop his friend from acting strangely.

They reached the end of the river of sewage. A grate of thick, metal bars blocked the way. Water could flow through, but there was no way a boy, even a small one, could escape through those heavy, iron bars.

"Even the sewer's a prison," Victor muttered.

"We could saw these bars open," Ratface said. "I've got a nail file we could try."

"That'd take a lifetime," Sully said. "Even with real tools it would take forever."

"Never mind," Carlos told them. "I'll just get back to work on my communicator device. That's the best way to get out of here—to send a message home and have our parents come get us. It's the middle of winter. If we bust out now, we'd freeze to death before we got far."

Sully tapped his forehead. "There's something we're forgetting," he said. "Remember what Nurse Bilgewater said to the things in the pitcher? She said she'd come visit them soon. And she said that whatever they were would have friends to play with."

"So?" Ratface said. "So what?"

"So," Sully replied, "She's not dumping whatever it is into the sewers. I think she's dumping something into some other place."

"And if she's going to visit it soon," Cody said, "the only way to figure out where she's dumping stuff is to follow her there."

"Maybe," Victor said. "But will it lead to a way out of here?"

They hurried back to class and sat through another afternoon of Fronk's tentacles writing assignments on the chalkboard. They had to do actual math problems that day. It was horrible.

When classes broke for dinner, the boys shuffled out the classroom door.

"Anybody want tuna fish for supper?" Mugsy asked.

"Quiet, fish face," Victor said. "What's with you?"

"What I want to know is why is Bilgewater keeping creatures she's not supposed to against Farley's wishes?" Cody asked. "And why does Dr. Farley want her to get rid of them?"

"And there are apparently lots of them," Sully added. Then he paused. They heard a creaking sound and footsteps coming down the hall. "Someone's coming. It's Bilgewater."

"C'mon," Ratface whispered. "Let's get to the bottom of this. Let's spy on her."

"She'll fish-fry us if she catches us," Sully warned.

"Nah," Cody said. "Don't be scared."

They hid against a dark wall where they could spy on her.

Bilgewater came into view, pushing her wheelbarrow down the hall. Something large and wet and dark was inside the wheelbarrow, with long, curling arms reaching up and out of it, reaching for her hat, her collar . . .

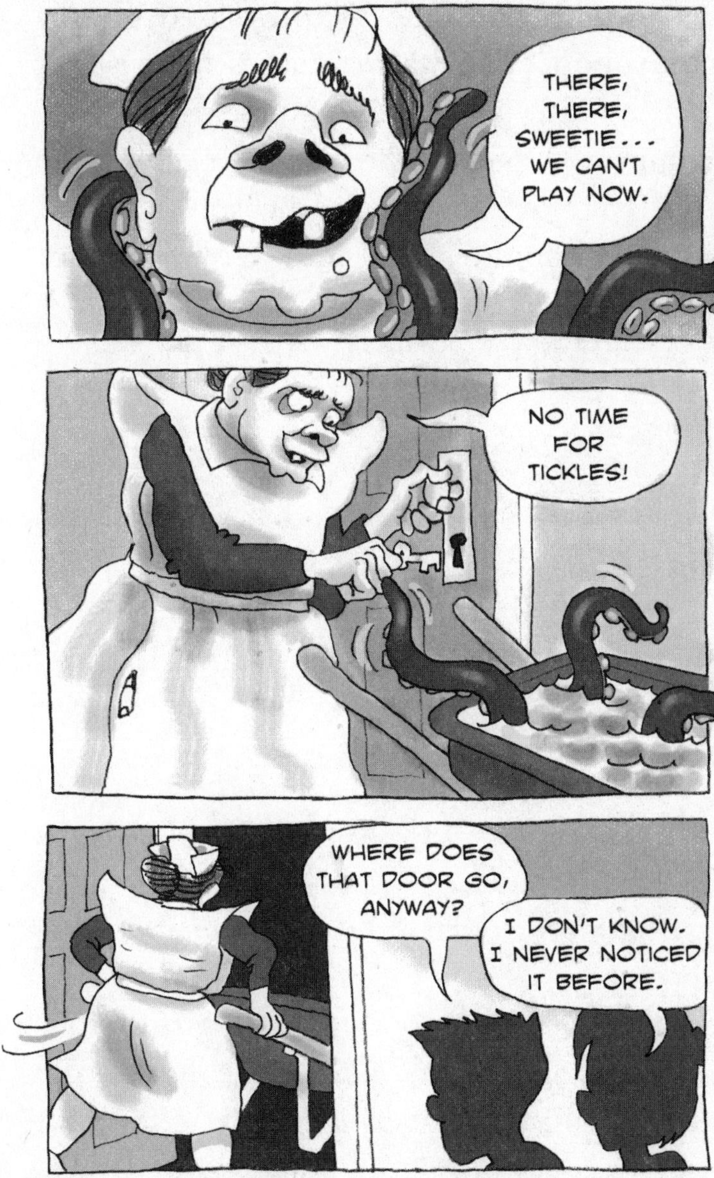
THERE, THERE, SWEETIE . . . WE CAN'T PLAY NOW.
NO TIME FOR TICKLES!
WHERE DOES THAT DOOR GO, ANYWAY?
I DON'T KNOW. I NEVER NOTICED IT BEFORE.

Seconds later, they heard a loud splash. Cody noticed a warm, damp, fishy smell wafting down the hall. Nurse Bilgewater reappeared, pushing an empty wheelbarrow.

"Bye-bye, tootsie," Bilgewater called over her shoulder. "I'll come feed you more tonight."

CHAPTER SEVEN

THE POOL

"An underground water tank! That's what it has to be," Cody told Carlos that night in their freezing cold dorm room. "We've got to get down there."

Snow lashed against the windows. Drifts had blown under the stable doors. A glass of water Mugsy had left by his stall the night before was frozen solid.

Carlos was busy wiring his communicator gizmo from the smashed-up guts of Fronk's cell phone. He'd swiped a soldering gun from Professor Eelpot's lab and a roll of lead solder, which he was melting onto the circuit boards. Cody watched him work.

"How're you coming on your walkie-talkie-cell-phone thingy, Carlos?" Victor asked. "Is it ready to call for help?"

"Close," Carlos said. "Tomorrow I'll borrow some batteries from the science room, and then we'll see."

"BOYS TALKING AFTER HOURS WILL BE FED TO PAVLOV," came Miss Threadbare's screechy voice over the intercom. "GO TO SLEEP IF YOU KNOW WHAT'S GOOD FOR YOU."

Cody crawled under his pile of straw. "Nothing here is good for you," he muttered.

When they arrived in science class the next day, the room stunk like a garbage barge on a hot summer day. Professor Eelpot began class with an announcement. "You didn't put your dissecting specimens away properly yesterday," she said in her soft voice. "They needed refrigeration. Instead, they rotted, and I had to give them to Griselda to use in tonight's stroganoff."

Victor paled, but Mugsy licked his lips.

Nobody did. Except Sully, of course. Sully knew everything. But Sully didn't speak around adults. Cody and the other boys stared at the hideous, massive-jawed fish that lurked in a lower corner of its dark tank.

"*No one* knows what angling is?" Professor Eelpot sounded like a purring cat waiting to pounce on a trapped mouse.

Cody saw Sully making secret little gestures. He flicked his right wrist forward, then with his left hand spun an imaginary wheel. It was as if he was playing charades with Cody.

"Fishing?" Cody guessed aloud.

"That's right," Professor Eelpot said. "*Angling* means *fishing*. The anglerfish uses a little fishing lure, attached to her forehead, to attract fish and eat them. Some species, like this one, have a lure that glows in the dark."

"You mean this fish fishes for other fish?" Ratface said. "That's sick."

"Not at all," Professor Eelpot said, staring at Ratface with one of her dark-rimmed eyes. "In the ocean, it's eat or be eaten. Survival is all that matters. Most anglerfish live at very great ocean depths, deep down, where the sunlight can't reach. It's cold down there, and there's not much oxygen in the water. The deeper the water, the stranger the creatures. Watch."

She unsealed a small plastic bag containing a little goldfish and dumped it into the tank. The goldfish ignored the anglerfish, but when the angler lit up its lure like a spaghetti noodle protruding from its forehead, the curious goldfish wiggled its way over to investigate.

"The moral of this story, class," Professor Eelpot said, "is, in your life, which would you rather be? The anglerfish or the goldfish? Think about it."

The boys stared at her. Cody shook his head in disbelief.

"Isn't it obvious?" Ratface said. "We don't have a choice. We're stuck here at Splurch Academy. We're total goldfish."

Professor Eelpot smiled broadly and winked at Ratface. "I know."

The bell rang, and they rose to leave.

Cody felt like he couldn't get out of that room fast enough. They hurried down the hall toward the cafeteria. On the way they found Miss Threadbare chewing Nurse Bilgewater out about something. Normally Bilgewater would never have put up with that, but she barely seemed to be listening today.

DON'T LET YOURSELF FALL TO PIECES, BEULAH! YOU'RE GETTING FAR TOO WORKED UP OVER...

YOINK

Cody's heart pounded. He wanted to get away before Bilgewater and Threadbare realized the keys were missing—which would draw attention to them. They walked slowly around the corner and out of sight.

"Where do we go now? Lunch?" Mugsy asked. "Sea slug stroganoff! Yum!"

"C'mon, Mugsy," Cody said. "We're going to go see what's behind that door Bilgewater went into earlier. Remember?"

"Who cares about that?" Carlos demanded. "Let's test this phone! I've got the batteries rigged in. Let's call home and request a fast taxi ride out of this place!"

"Not a taxi," Victor said. "A helicopter."

"A stealth bomber," Ratface said. "Come swooping in here before Farley can even hear its engines. Then, when we're gone, blow the place to bits!"

They reached the empty classroom and slipped inside. Carlos whipped out his phone and began dialing numbers. "I almost don't remember my home phone number," he said. He was so nervous and excited his fingers shook. "It's beeping. The batteries are working. That's a good sign. There! Dial." He finished and held the phone up to his ear expectantly.

YEAH? WHO'S THAT? WHO'S THERE?

MOM? DAD?

SCHPEAK UP, SONNY! I AIN'T NOBODY'S MOM OR DAD. YOU MUSTA CALLED THE WRONG NUMBER.

I DON'T UNDERSTAND. I DIALED MY HOME NUMBER EXACTLY RIGHT.

"Hang up and let me try." Cody took the phone and punched in his own number, checking to make sure he'd dialed correctly.

"Pinky's Recycled Lubricants, can I help you?" a woman's voice replied.

"Come again? What?"

"This is Pinky's Recycled Lubricants in Milwaukee, Wisconsin," the secretary said. "Nobody greases your skids the second time around quite like Pinky's. With whom do you wish to speak?"

"Never mind." Cody hung up. He handed the phone back to Carlos, who shook his head.

"I must have wired the numbers wrong," Carlos said.

"Either that or our families have all left the country," Cody said, patting him on the back. "Never mind. You'll fix it. C'mon, let's see what's behind this door."

Ratface stuck the key in the lock and cranked it. The door swung open to a dark room. Echoes bounced off the walls, and a warm, fishy smell rose from near the floor.

"You guys stay here and stand guard," Cody said. "I'll check it out."

"Don't go in there, Cody," Ratface whimpered. "What if whatever's in there can suck your eyeballs out through its nostrils?"

Cody took one step forward, then another. His eyes took a while to adjust to the near-darkness.

Cody climbed out of the pool. The other boys slipped and fell, too, landing in a damp and dirty heap near the edge of the pool. They got up, rubbed their bruises, and looked around.

The pool chamber was dimly lit by small fluorescent lamps at the exits. The air stunk worse than before as the dark water sloshed gently against the edges of the pool.

"There's something in the water, Cody," Sully said. "See? Little somethings moving."

Carlos and Cody knelt down beside Sully for a better look.

"Are you sure?" Cody said. "I don't see anything."

Sully leaned out over the water and pointed. "What do you think Bilgewater's been dumping in here, cookie crumbs? Of course there's something living in here. Look."

They knelt to examine the dark surface of the water. Suddenly Mugsy became excited. He plowed in between them and pushed the other boys aside.

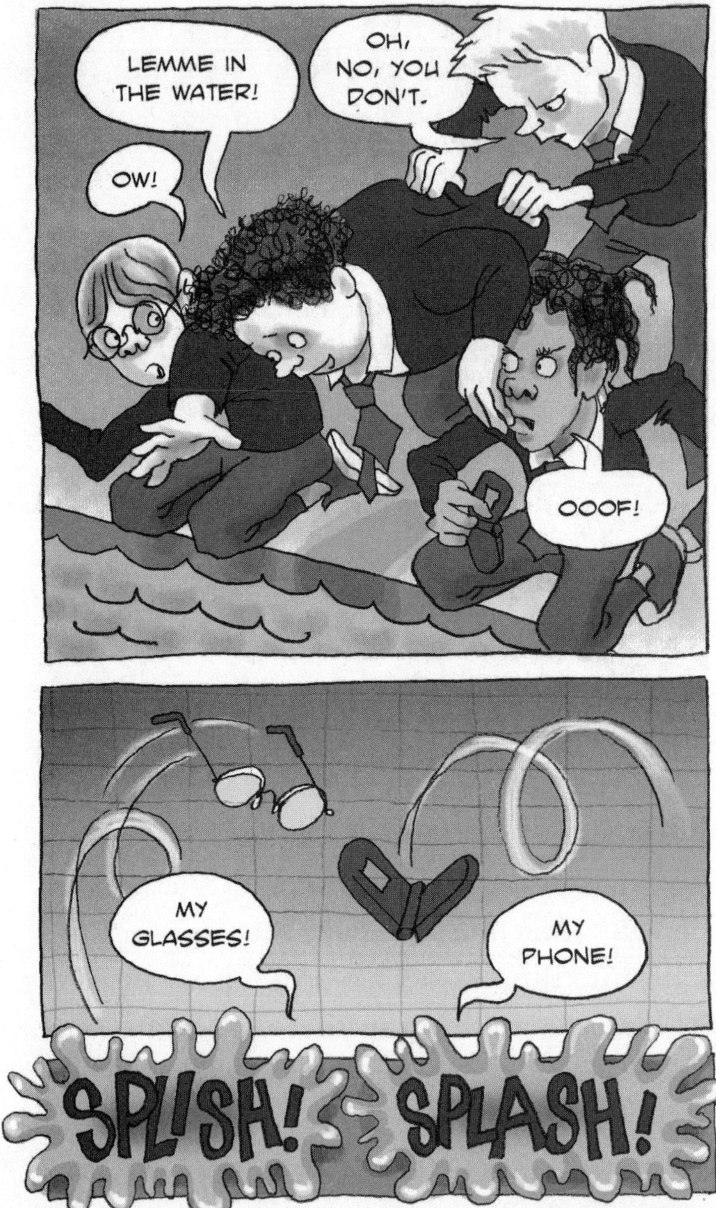
LEMME IN THE WATER!
OH, NO, YOU DON'T.
OW!
OOOF!
MY GLASSES!
MY PHONE!
SPLISH! SPLASH!

CHAPTER EIGHT

THE SQUID

Cody reached in the water and grabbed for the phone and the glasses. No luck.

"How will we ever get home without my phone?" Carlos moaned.

"That phone was a crazy gamble from the beginning," Sully snapped. "Without my glasses, I'm as blind as a jellyfish!"

Cody reached in again, and this time he felt something brush his arm. "Ew," he said. "There's something in there, all right." He fished around more but felt no sign of the phone or the glasses. But when he pulled his arm up . . .

They got the slimy, wriggling thing off
Cody's arm. Victor held it out for all to see.
Its tentacled arms reached for him. "That's
a squid," he said. "My uncle took me ocean
fishing once, and we caught one."

"My mom took me to a Chinese
restaurant once, and I ate one," Ratface said.
"But I never knew they looked like that."

"Squids in a swimming pool?" Carlos
said. "Why?"

"This must be what Nurse Bilgewater's
been dumping," Sully said. "I wonder how
many of them there are in the pool."

Victor grabbed a pool net from the wall. "I'll find your glasses, Sully," he said.

He plunged the net into the water. Down, down it went, till Victor was holding the handle by its very end. "It still hasn't touched the bottom," he said.

They trotted over to investigate. Cody pulled Sully by the arm so he wouldn't slip into the water. Without his glasses, he was helpless.

Ratface held up his discovery. "It's like something from a museum," he said. "Look! Oxygen tanks and everything!"

"Looks pretty old," Carlos said. "Like a costume from an old sci-fi movie." His face was downcast. "Who cares about any of this stuff? Without my phone, we're still prisoners."

"The phone's probably ruined by the water, anyway," Sully said. "Forget the stupid phone. It's my glasses that matter."

"Whaddaya mean by 'stupid phone'?" Carlos retorted. "It was a brilliant idea! And I don't see you coming up with any escape plans."

"That's because I'm not an idiot!" Sully yelled. "I can face facts. We're stuck here forever until we get turned into monsters or turned into lunch. But I'd still like to be able to see. Farley sure won't buy me a replacement pair of glasses. That creepy, old vampire will probably be happy I'm as blind as a bat."

"What I don't get," Ratface said, "is what Farley's doing with a diving suit. We're miles and miles from any ocean. Plus I thought vampires hated water. What good is it to him?"

"It's good for us in one way," Cody said. "I'm gonna use that diving suit to go down and find the glasses and the phone." He started pulling the aqua suit on over his clothes. "Pee-yew, it stinks!"

"You can't go down there," Carlos said. "Are you scuba trained? Do you even know how to dog-paddle?

"Be careful down there, Cody," Victor said. "Don't drown."

"C'mon, it's a swimming pool," Cody said. "Ten feet deep, maximum. What can go wrong? If any teachers show up and you need me to come back, just yank on the breathing tube."

"Look, an underwater flashlight," Ratface said, switching it on. "With working batteries! That'll come in handy."

Cody fastened his helmet over his head. He felt like a goldfish in a bowl—for the second time today. He just hoped there weren't any anglerfish at the bottom of this pool waiting to eat him. He checked to make sure he could breathe, then tugged on the oxygen hose connecting him to the surface.

SLOWLY, SLOWLY HE SANK
INTO THE MURKY DARKNESS.

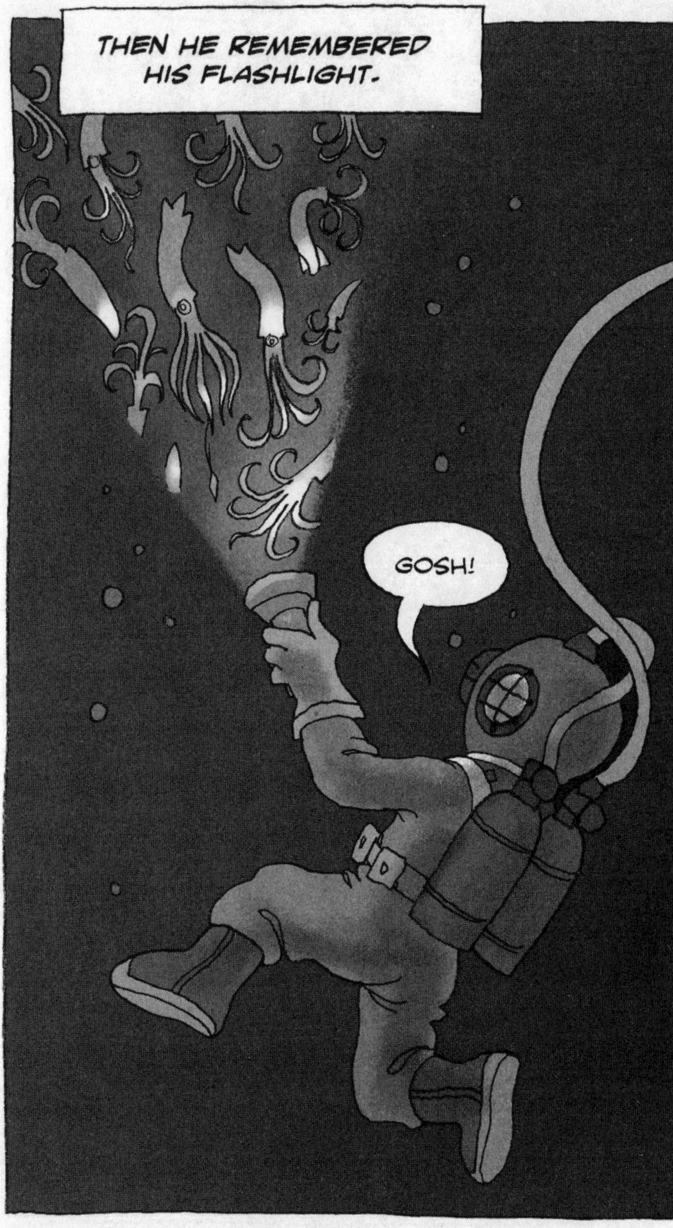
THEN HE REMEMBERED HIS FLASHLIGHT.
GOSH!

Cody windmilled his arms and legs to try to swim. He shone the flashlight down. No sign of a bottom to this pool. Just swimming squids for as far as the eye could see. He shone it up, but there was no way to tell how deep he'd gone. *At least I'm still connected to the surface. But how will I ever find Sully's glasses in all this water?*

He shone the light around. Then something caught his eye. It was Carlos's phone, with lights still flashing. Cody aimed his flashlight toward it. A squid was holding the phone! The squid was even bigger than he was! Cody swam over to where the squid hovered in the water. The creepy creature was actually trying to punch buttons on the phone with one of its pointy arms! And wrapped around its tubular head were Sully's glasses!

Cody grabbed for the squid, but it pushed him away with its powerful arms and shot, torpedo style, across the pool. Shoot. He should have thought first before alerting the squid to his presence. Boy, that was one smart squid, pressing buttons just like a person! Was this typical squid behavior? Cody didn't think so. Why would a squid try to wear glasses?

Cody swam in pursuit. The squid appeared to have forgotten about Cody. It hovered upside down, still probing the phone with its wiggly arms. Cody snuck up behind it and grabbed one of its arms, yanking hard. The squid swam off, taking the phone and Sully's glasses with him.

Finally Cody reached the bottom of the pool and retreived Sully's glasses.

CHAPTER NINE

THE CAVE

"Is Cody okay down there?" Ratface asked. "Should we haul him up?"

"It's taking him a long time," Sully said. "Please, oh please, oh please, find my glasses!"

"The tube is still moving around," Victor pointed out. "That must mean Cody is, too. And if he's moving, then he must be okay."

"I wish there was some way to see what he's up to," Carlos said.

"Quit bragging about seeing," Sully muttered.

Just then, overhead, the pool lights flipped on. Footsteps echoed across the pool deck. A familiar voice broke the silence. "What in the name of Jupiter?"

"Bilgewater!" Ratface warned. "Quick, everybody hide!"

Meanwhile, down at the bottom of the deep pool, Cody had a decision to make. The squid had disappeared through the crack in the pool floor. Cody wanted to go after it and explore what was under the crack. *It must be big if the squid can swim right through. We need that phone,* he thought. *It's our only chance to get out of here.* Still, there was no telling where this crack might lead. It could go to some kind of vicious sea monster's lair. *Don't be silly,* Cody thought. *It's not like I'm in a hurry. I've got a breathing tube. I could stay down here for hours. What's the harm in exploring?*

Cody yanked on his oxygen hose to make sure there was plenty of length available. *It's just a crack in a pool,* he thought. *How big can it be? I'll catch that squid in no time.*

Cody decided to take the plunge. He took a deep breath, held tight to Sully's glasses, and dived down through the crack.

It was even darker down there. The beam from his flashlight seemed puny, and it faded before it ever found an edge to the hole. The temperature felt colder through his suit.

What is this place? Cody thought. *The water goes on and on forever! This is one seriously leaky pool.*

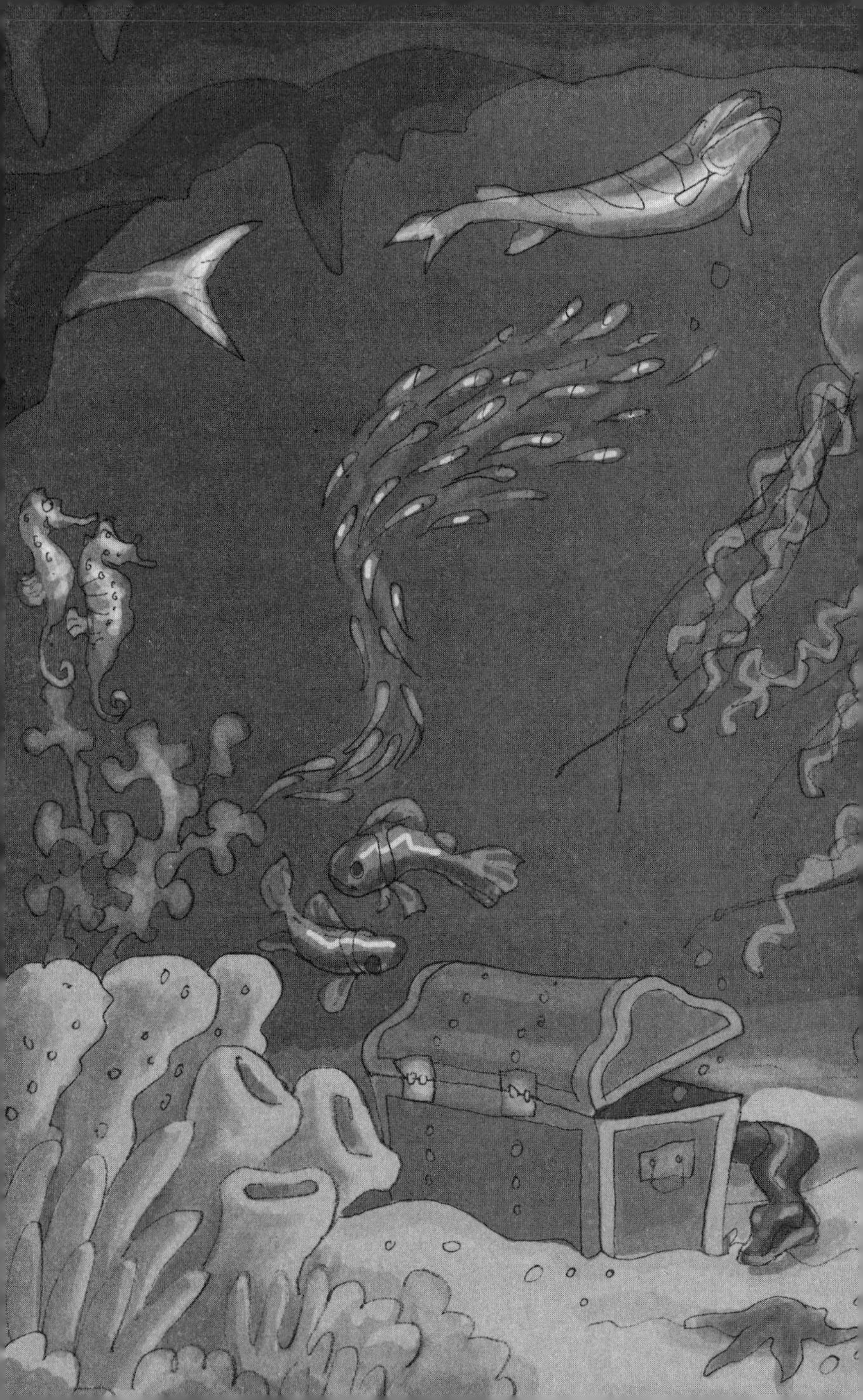

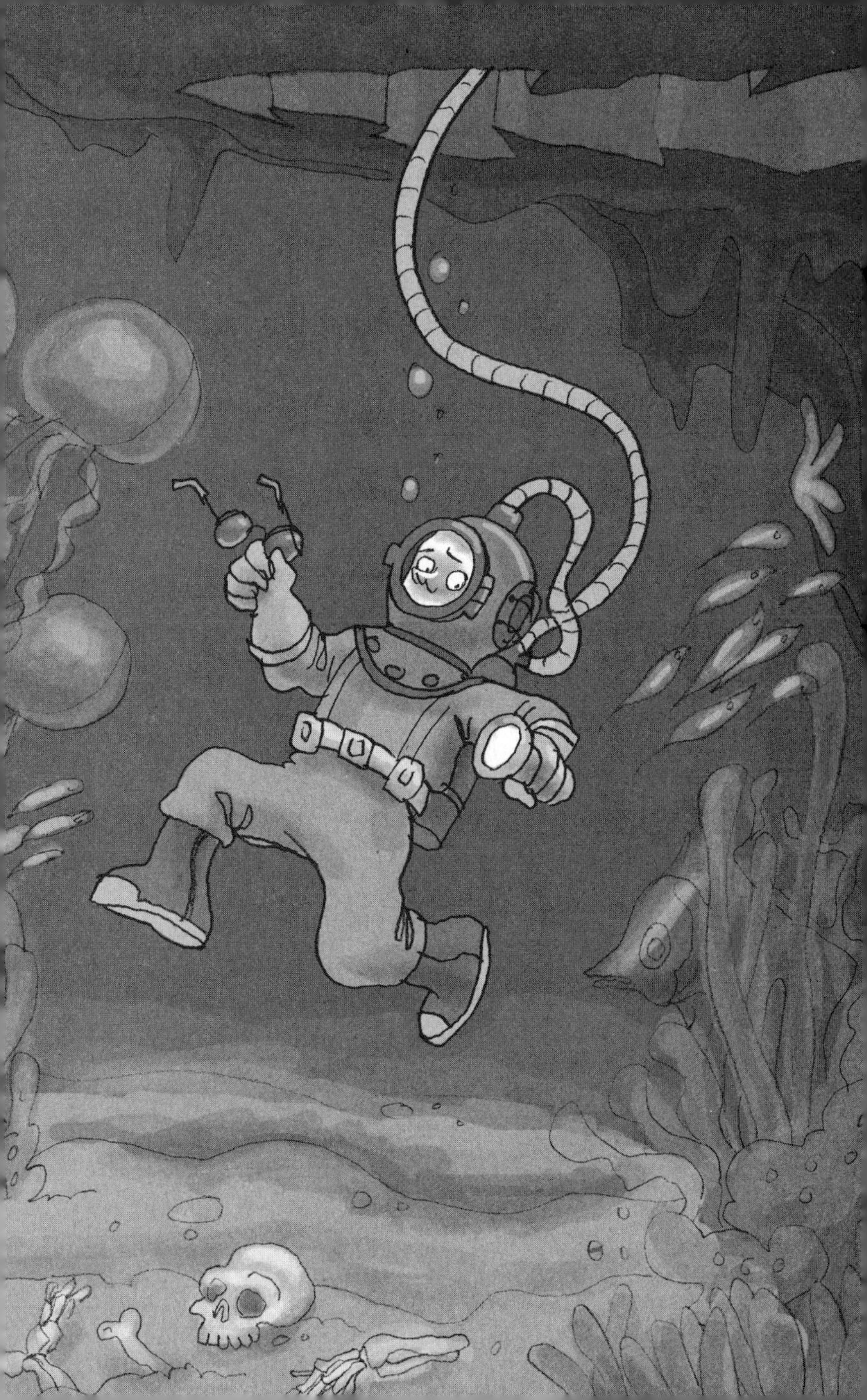

A treasure chest! With gold coins! Cody felt around to see if his suit had any pockets. It didn't.

Small fish by the dozens swam over to Cody to investigate his flashlight. *Just like the anglerfish*, he thought. *It must always be dark down here. This is maybe the first light they've ever seen!* Just then, a floating, glowing school of pink jellyfish bobbed by. No, there were other things that glowed down here, too. Cody was glad he had a suit on to protect him from the stinging jellies.

The floor of the underwater cave was like a gigantic fish tank. There was still no sign of the squid with the cell phone. Then Cody saw a greenish light in the distance. *It might be the phone,* he thought. He set off to investigate.

It was no mere cell phone. This was something big looming in the distance. A sea monster? Cody approached cautiously.

When he got closer, he dropped his flashlight in astonishment.

It was a submarine! With lights on inside!

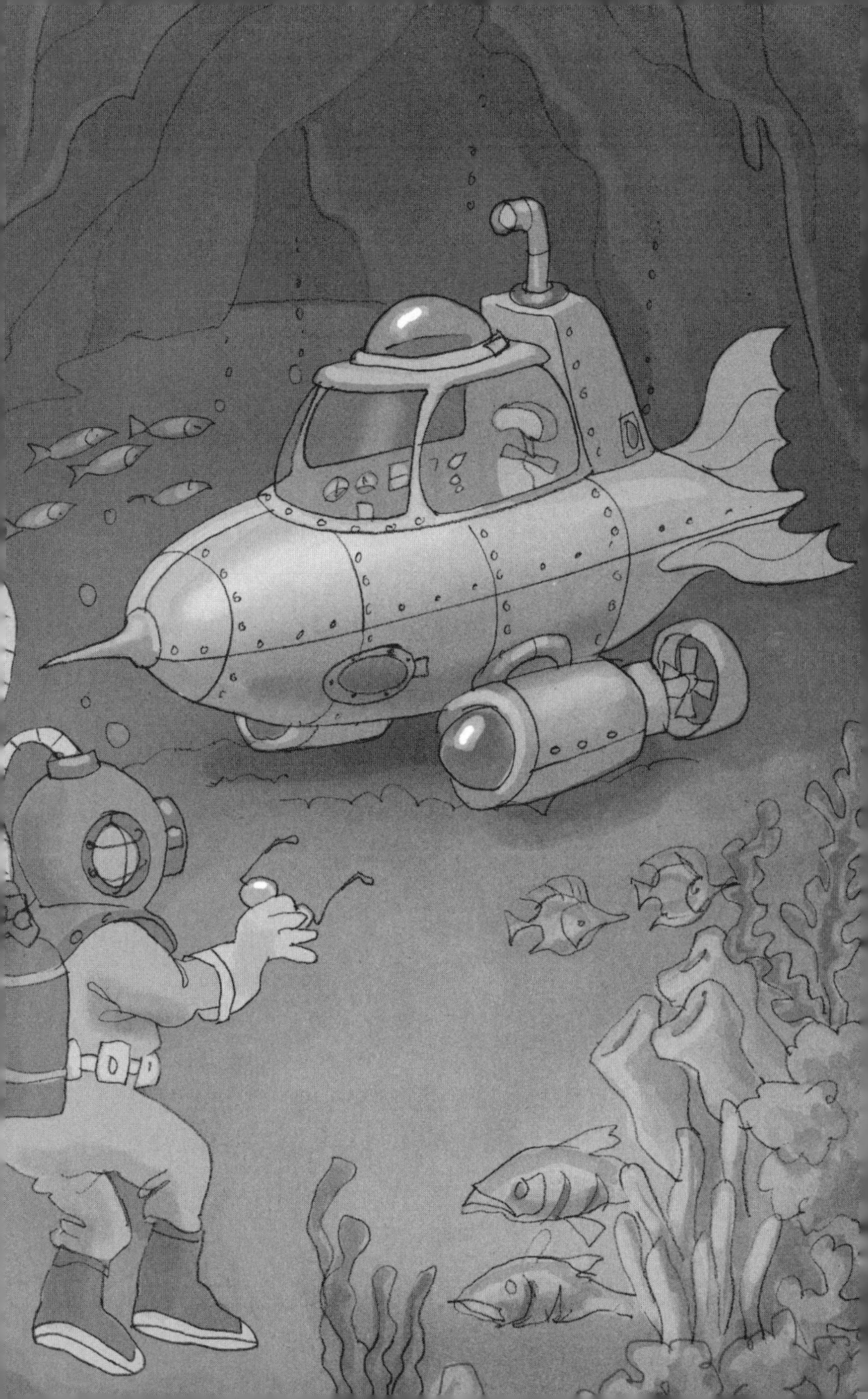

Cody peered through the windows. Who could have left a submarine here? Why would someone have a submarine underneath the broken, abandoned swimming pool?

Cody's mind started spinning. All this water under here had to have come from the ocean. Shipwrecks, jellyfish . . . there was no other explanation. This *was* an underground ocean cave, maybe, mysteriously reaching for miles, all the way to Splurch Academy. And here was a *submarine*. Never mind cell phones . . . this was a real way out! Somehow, if he could just get everybody down here, they could sail away under the sea to freedom!

Bilgewater's sensible nursing shoes clicked across the pool deck. She sniffed the air, her nostrils flaring wide. She carried a huge pail of mackerel. She grabbed one and munched it like a candy bar. Then she tipped her pail into the pool.

"All right, come out," she called. "Where are you? I know there are stinking boys down here somewhere."

Then Nurse Bilgewater caught sight of the breathing tube running down into the pool.

"Aha," she cried. "Something fishy's going on here."

She reached down, grabbed the tube, and yanked it.

Ratface gasped. Victor clamped a hand over his mouth. "That's the signal!" Ratface breathed. "Cody's gonna come to the surface now. She'll catch him!"

Moments before, down at the bottom of the cave, Cody was still peering at the submarine when the squid with the cell phone went gliding past him. He turned and aimed his flashlight at it. In one arm it held the cell phone. In another it held . . . an old ketchup bottle! How weird!

Cody followed the departing creature with his flashlight. Then his heart thumped in his chest. It was only a shadowy movement. He couldn't be sure. But something larger—much larger than the cell phone squid—swam past the beam of his light.

Was that a ship? A *whale*? Or could Cody simply be imagining things down here in the murky depths?

Maybe it was time to get out of here.

Just then he felt a sharp tug from the breathing tube.

"Geez, guys," he muttered to himself. "Tug any harder, and it'll come off. Then I'd drown down here!"

Kicking, swimming, and climbing up the tube, hand over hand, Cody made his way toward the surface.

Nurse Bilgewater suddenly turned toward where the boys were hiding. She was inches away from discovering them. They could smell her fishy body odor and mackerel breath.

LITTLE BOOOOYS...
I CAN HEEEAAR
YOU!

SOMETHING WET FLOPPED OUT OF THE POOL AND LANDED AT NURSE BILGEWATER'S FEET.

HUH?

OH, THERE YOU ARE, PUMPKIN! I WAS WORRIED ABOUT YOU.

She reached down and tickled the squid. "Where's your big brother?" she asked. "Is he still being mean to you? The big bully! I'll give him a talking-to. But first, I have some business to attend to." She pulled a long, sinister-looking pair of scissors from her nurse's uniform pocket and seized the breathing tube. "Choppity chop!"

The boys, watching from behind the box, froze in terror. What about Cody? If she cut the tube, he'd drown down there!

"Whoever's down there in the water isn't supposed to be," she said, loud enough for all the boys to hear. "If there's one thing I hate, it's rule breakers."

"We've got to stop her," Carlos whispered. "We've got to save Cody!"

Just then a figure emerged from the shadows and spoke.

"Except when you're the rule breaker. Isn't that right, Beulah?"

Nurse Bilgewater whipped around to see the newcomer. She rose to her feet, brandishing the scissors.

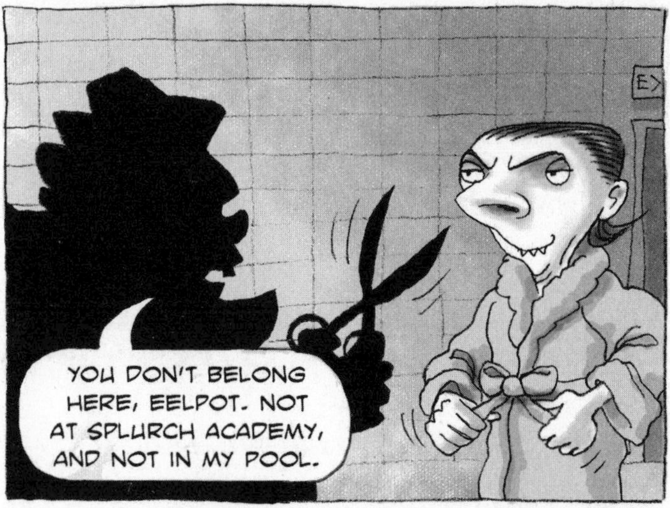
EX
YOU DON'T BELONG HERE, EELPOT. NOT AT SPLURCH ACADEMY, AND NOT IN MY POOL.

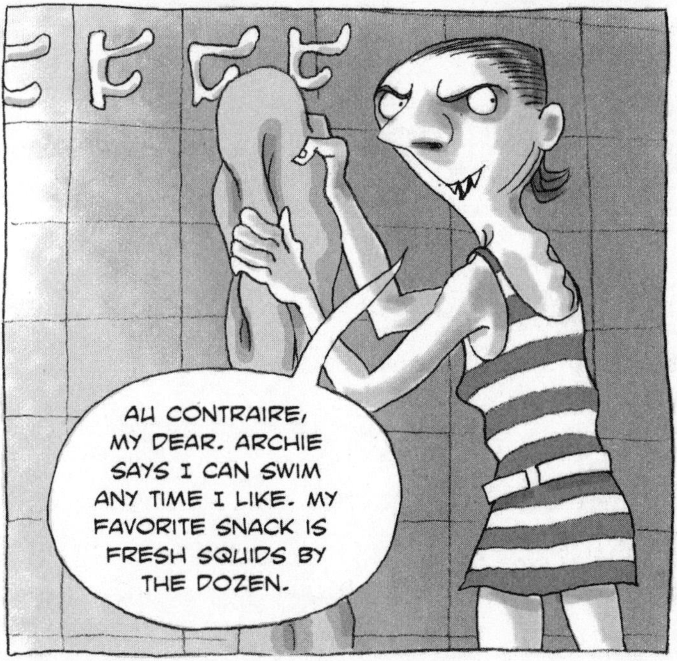
AU CONTRAIRE, MY DEAR. ARCHIE SAYS I CAN SWIM ANY TIME I LIKE. MY FAVORITE SNACK IS FRESH SQUIDS BY THE DOZEN.

Bilgewater's face crumpled with rage. "So *you're* the one chomping my baby squiddies!" she screamed. "Vertebrate vermin!"

Eelpot laughed and flexed her arm muscles. "Don't blow a gasket, cephalopod scum! I wonder what Farley will say when I tell him you're hiding squids down here in the pool." She shook her head . . . *and transformed into a shark woman!*

She chomped her jaws and dived into the pool.

Bilgewater ripped off her nurse's hat and shoes. "Oh, no, you don't, you fishy fiend! You're not gonna munch on my squiddies!" As she spoke, Bilgewater's legs dissolved into fat, oily octopus tentacle arms.

"Gross," Ratface whispered to Sully. "Do all girls do that?"

Sully clapped a hand over Ratface's mouth.

With a colossal splash, Nurse Bilgewater heaved herself over the edge of the pool and into the water, chasing after Eelpot.

Just then Cody's bubble diving helmet bobbed up to the surface. He climbed out of the pool and popped the helmet off his head.

"Hey! Guys!" he said. "Sully, I got your glasses. You'll never guess what's down there!"

Sully grabbed the glasses gratefully. "You're my hero, man," he said.

The other boys attacked Cody, unzipping him out of his suit before he could protest.

"*You'll* never guess what's down there," Victor said. "But we don't have time to tell you now. Unless you want to be fish food, hurry up. Let's get outta here!"

CHAPTER TEN

THE MUTANT

"I'm telling you, guys, it's a working sub," Cody said. "Probably nuclear powered and everything. It's all ready to get us outta here once and for all!"

They were huddled around a little fire they'd built on the floor of the stables. Ratface had stolen firewood from the teachers' lounge and matches and a package of marshmallows from the kitchen. They had to be careful because the stables were full of straw, and if one strand caught fire, the boys would all be charred like cheap hot dogs. Hot dogs . . . too bad they didn't have any of *those* to roast over the fire. Boys at Splurch Academy were always hungry. Griselda's cooking made sure of that. A hot dog with ketchup and mustard sure would hit the spot . . . never mind. When they reached home they'd get to have all the hot dogs they wanted.

At Carlos's instruction, the boys were attempting to lash snowshoes out of sticks and straw. Carlos, who was always good at making things, was doing a decent job of making his, but Cody's and everyone else's looked like bad birds' nests. Cody humored Carlos, though, because he knew his friend was still sore about the lost cell phone.

Carlos's new plan was that they'd all escape over the snow using their snowshoes, but Cody knew that was a long shot. The teachers would track them down in no time. On the other hand, sailing away through a hidden ocean cave . . . that was a whole different matter.

"That sub is our ticket home," he said aloud.

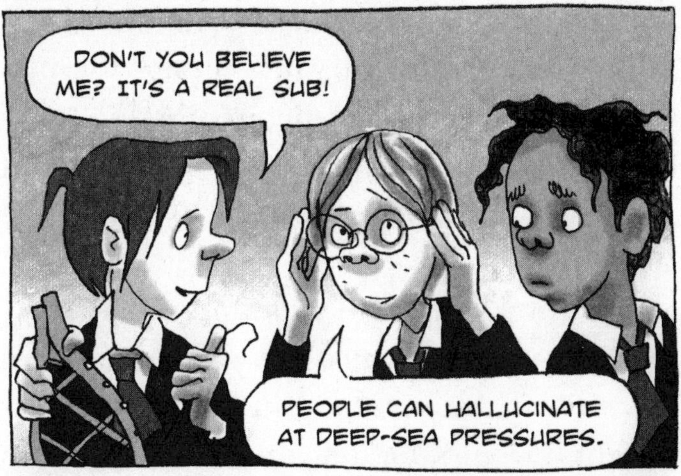
DON'T YOU BELIEVE ME? IT'S A REAL SUB!
PEOPLE CAN HALLUCINATE AT DEEP-SEA PRESSURES.

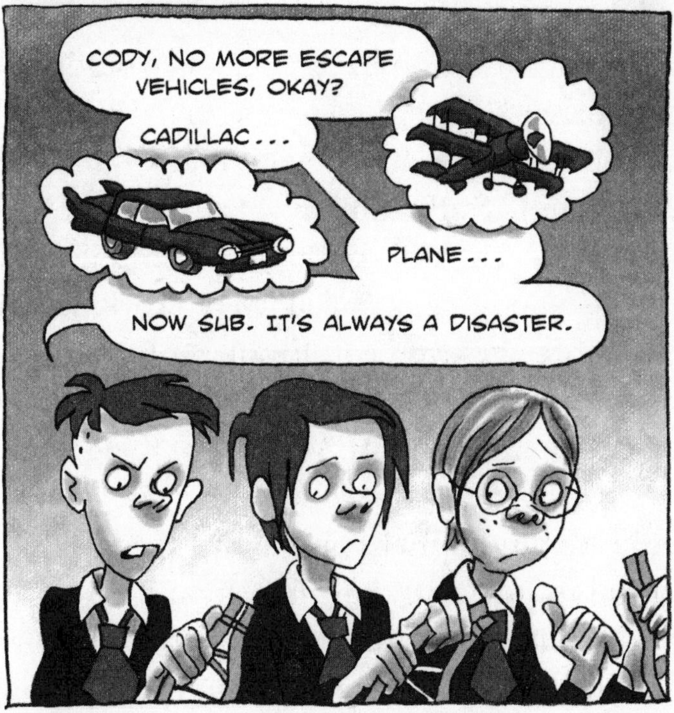
CODY, NO MORE ESCAPE VEHICLES, OKAY?
CADILLAC . . .
PLANE . . .
NOW SUB. IT'S ALWAYS A DISASTER.

Cody's friends all stared at him bleakly.

"It was a nice thought, though." Sully patted Cody's knee encouragingly. "The main thing is you found my glasses. That was your *important* discovery under the water."

"If only you could've found my phone," Carlos said, his voice full of anger. "I'd have fixed the numbers in a jiffy, and our parents would be on their way here to rescue us right now."

"Not in this blizzard, they wouldn't," Victor said.

"I doubt the phone would have survived the water," Sully said.

"You can still build a communicator, 'Los," Cody said. "You were working on it before we ever got Fronk's phone. Just go back to your original plan. With the chandeliers and stuff."

Carlos didn't look consoled at all. He dropped more sticks on the fire. Sparks flew up in the air, and they all watched carefully to see where they'd land.

"Oh, hey," Ratface said. "Forgot to show

you this. I swiped it off the front hall table today after the mail arrived." He showed them a postcard of an ancient Greek temple. "It's from the Priscilla Prim girls."

Hey, stupid Splurch Boys,
Having a great time in Greece.
Discovered a lost shrine to a Greek god. Wish you were here. NOT!

Signed,
the Girls

5th Grade Boys
Splurch Academy
13 Belladonna Dr.
Splurchville

"Hmph," Ratface grumbled. "I'll bet they didn't even discover some dumb Greek shrine."

"Those annoying girls," Victor fumed. "I'm so glad they're gone."

"Especially Virginia," Cody said. "She's the worst. Thinks she rules the world."

They sat staring at the fire, thinking

about sunny Mediterranean beaches and feeling miserable.

"Hey, Mugsy," Cody said. "You're not saying much."

Mugsy shrugged.

"Not feeling well or something?" Cody asked.

But Mugsy only grunted.

"The snow's stopped," Sully observed.

"You realize what that means?" Cody said. "All the monsters will be out hunting again tonight. We could go check out the pool again, and if we find a way into the sub, we can break free tonight!"

Ratface ignored Cody. He stood and rubbed a pajama sleeve on a frost-covered windowpane. "Look! There's the moon," he said. "It's kinda pretty on the snow."

They all stood and gathered around to look out the window.

"It's just like the holidays," Carlos whispered. "Makes me want cookies."

"It's . . . HOLY CALAMARI!" Ratface shrieked. "Guys! Look at Mugsy!"

They turned toward their friend. He

looked sick. Then he looked like something that would make *them* sick.

His body twitched, his face convulsed. His fingers clenched and clawed the air. The legs of his pants shredded and ripped apart as eight giant tentacle arms appeared where his legs had been.

"Yikes!" Ratface squealed. "Something gross ate Mugsy's legs!"

"Say something, man!" Victor yelled. "Does it hurt?"

Carlos elbowed the others aside. "He wasn't eaten. He's turning into an octo-boy!" he said. "Like Nurse Bilgewater."

Sully shook his head. "She's part octopus, but Mugsy is part squid."

"We've got to make it stop!" Cody cried. "This is Mugsy we're talking about. We've got to fix him! Get him back to normal."

"But how?" Ratface said. "How could this have happened?" He patted himself all over, making sure he still had human legs. "Are we all next?"

Mugsy, meanwhile, was having trouble standing on his squid legs. He kept skidding and slithering around and collapsing to the floor.

"Speak to me, Mugsy," Cody cried. "Are you okay? Are you still in there?"

"If he keeps falling like that, he's going to break all his bones," Carlos said.

"Cephalopods don't have bones," Sully said. "Mugsy may not have any, either. In fact, the cool thing about them is that they're so incredibly squishy, even the big ones can squeeze their bodies through the tiniest openings."

They propped him upright to keep him from falling.

Sully frowned. "This is serious," he said. "We're losing him."

"What do we do?" Victor said. "We sure can't ask the teachers for help."

"Right," Cody said. "Farley can never know about this. We've got to keep him a secret."

"Uh, Cody," Ratface said, "this is going

to be pretty hard to hide. Mugsy, get your tentacles off me!"

Cody paced the floor. "Farley must have done this. But how? What's going on? What are the clues? What do we know? C'mon, everybody, think."

They sat around the dwindling fire, trying to think and trying to keep Mugsy's suckered arms from picking their noses.

"What about Professor Eelpot?" Carlos said. "She's a sea creature monster. Everything started getting all fishy around the time she showed up."

"She might be involved," Cody said, nodding.

"What about Professor Fronk?" Ratface said. "Mugsy's not the only one turning squiddy."

"Remember?" Carlos said. "When we were in the teachers' lounge and Dr. Farley pressured Mr. Fronk to participate in his experiment?"

"It must have something to do with genetics," Sully said. "The only way I can think of to turn a human into a squid is to swap out part of their DNA."

"Swap?" Cody said. His mind was spinning. "You mean put squid DNA in a person and put human DNA in a squid?"

Sully blinked. "I don't know what Farley does with the old human DNA. Wouldn't he just throw it out?"

Cody jumped up, knocking Mugsy back onto the floor. Mugsy had been trying to eat stable straw.

"When I was down in the pool," he exclaimed, "there was a squid following me around, playing with Carlos's phone, and carrying an old ketchup bottle!" He hoisted Mugsy back upright. "That squid must be part Mugsy!"

"You mean . . . there's two Mugsys now?" Ratface said.

"Sounds like it," Sully said. "One's a boy who's part squid, and one's a squid who's part boy."

"So which one's the real one?" Ratface demanded.

Sully scratched his head. "Both, I think."

"They've turned Mugsy into a monster," Victor moaned. "They've kidnapped him over to the dark side. He's one of them now. Not one of us. He may eat us in our sleep."

"We'll stay up keeping watch," Cody said. "This isn't Mugsy's fault. He's not one of them, he's still one of us. We've got to figure out a way to get him back to normal."

"What about the submarine idea?" Victor said. "You were right, Cody. With all the teachers outside hunting, now is our perfect chance to take the sub and get away. We could tie a leash on Mugsy and bring him along with us."

"What, and leave Mugsy a monster like this forever?" Cody said. "No. We've got to fix him. So first we've got to find out exactly what Farley's up to. Once we understand the science that mutated Mugsy, maybe we can mutate him back."

"Possibly," Sully said. "Or maybe, before we can figure out the secret, Farley will have mutated the rest of us."

CHAPTER ELEVEN
THE HAT

The next morning, Mugsy was back to his normal shape.

"Hot dog," Carlos said, giving Cody a high five. "He's his normal self again."

"You're back," Victor told Mugsy, giving him a hug that surprised everyone. "You came back!"

"Good thing, too," Carlos admitted to Cody on the way to breakfast. "It was my turn to keep watch over him, but I fell asleep. He could've eaten us all."

"I don't think that's what he's after," Cody said. "He's not monster enough yet."

Breakfast that morning was runny poached eggs on burned toast. Mugsy, who usually ate anything so long as it had ketchup, refused to touch his food. Then Farley appeared with a silver platter heaped with shiny pink shrimp surrounding a little goblet of red cocktail sauce.

"Can I interest you in a special breakfast this morning, Percival?" Farley cooed.

Mugsy's eyes grew wide. He snatched fistfuls of shrimps and popped them in his mouth whole, crunchy tails and all.

But Mugsy ignored him and just gobbled the shrimps right off the platter. Farley smiled down at Mugsy the whole time.

Cody glared at Farley, despising him. The headmaster patted Mugsy on his curly head and moved on.

"Why does he keep coming over here and looking at Mugsy funny?" Ratface muttered. "He's been doing that for days."

"He knows," Cody whispered to the other boys. "He knows about Mugsy."

"He knows what about Mugsy?" Mugsy muttered. "What's the deal?"

They stared at him and said nothing. Over in the corner of the cafeteria, Professor Eelpot approached Farley. She whispered in his ear. Their gazes both turned toward Nurse Bilgewater, who sat in one corner, cradling a coffee cup between her hands.

"I had the weirdest dream last night," Mugsy said. "I dreamed I was swimming in the ocean, but I was stuck in an underwater cave. I wanted to bust free to the big ocean, but I couldn't get out of the cave."

Cody and Carlos exchanged a look.

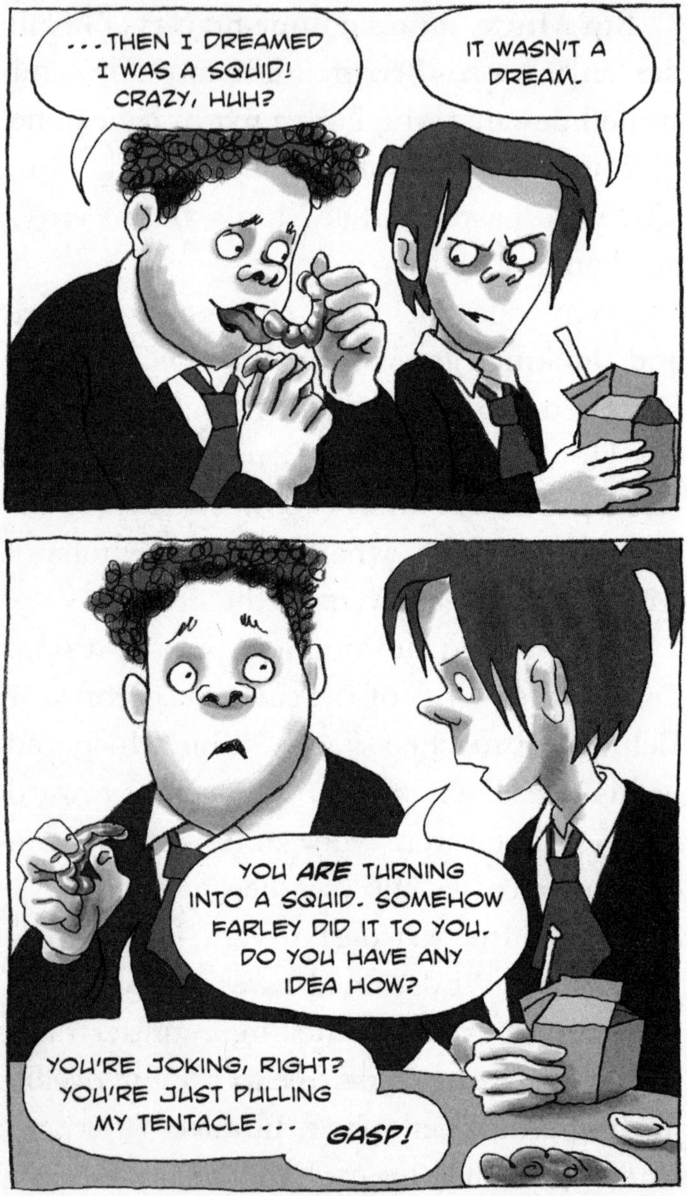
...THEN I DREAMED I WAS A SQUID! CRAZY, HUH?
IT WASN'T A DREAM.
YOU **ARE** TURNING INTO A SQUID. SOMEHOW FARLEY DID IT TO YOU. DO YOU HAVE ANY IDEA HOW?
YOU'RE JOKING, RIGHT? YOU'RE JUST PULLING MY TENTACLE...
GASP!

"It's time for us to get to class," Sully said. "Think, Mugsy. Think! Try and remember anything Farley might have done to you that made this happen, okay?"

Mugsy nodded. His eyes got red. "You're . . . gonna fix me, right?" he said. "You're not going to leave me this way, are you, guys? I don't want to be a fish!"

Sully raised a finger. "Technically, you're not a fish, you're a . . ." Victor elbowed him.

"Save the lesson for later," Victor said.

Poor Mugsy still looked so blue, Cody didn't know what to say. To his surprise, Victor put his arm around Mugsy's shoulders. "We're gonna do all we can, Mugs. Promise. Nobody turns my friends into octopuses without a fight."

Sully's finger went up once more. "Technically, though they're related, squids are not octopuses."

They headed to Mr. Fronk's class. There was their teacher, snoozing as usual. His legs had turned into tentacles and were feeling all over his desk, fiddling with pens and paper clips.

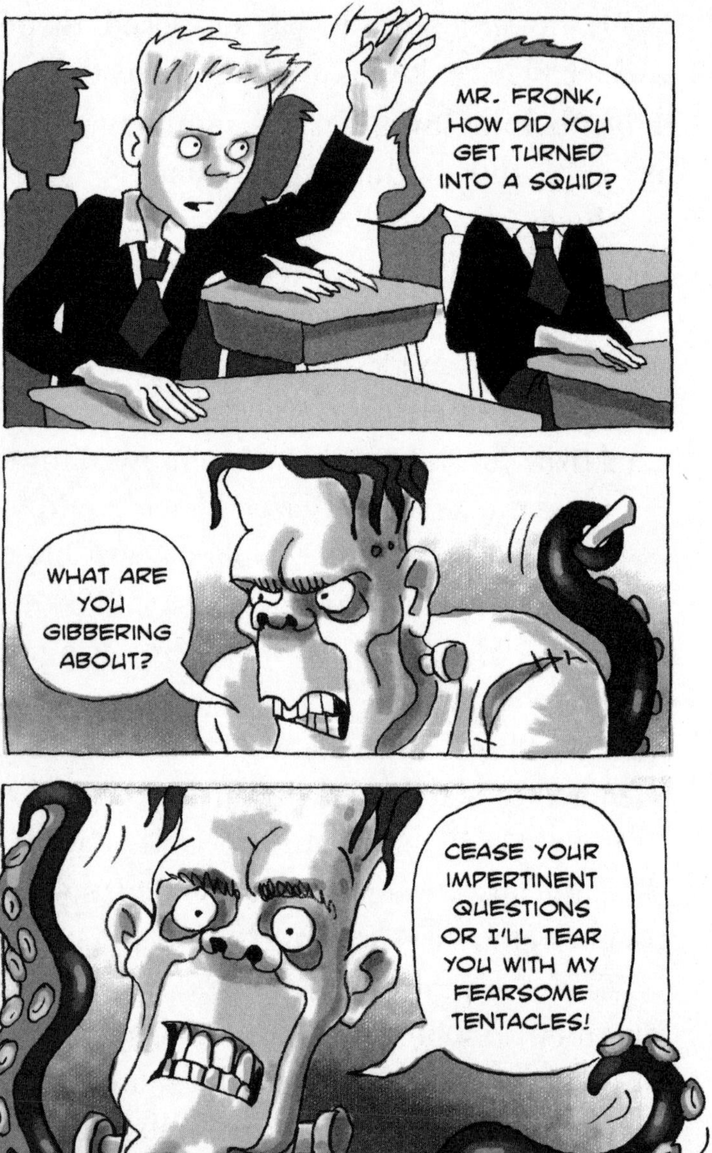
MR. FRONK, HOW DID YOU GET TURNED INTO A SQUID?
WHAT ARE YOU GIBBERING ABOUT?
CEASE YOUR IMPERTINENT QUESTIONS OR I'LL TEAR YOU WITH MY FEARSOME TENTACLES!

"I thought school was supposed to be a place where kids *could* ask questions," Ratface said. "Geez."

"How did Farley steal and swap your DNA," Carlos asked, "if you're made from body parts from lots of different people? I mean, you kinda came from the secondhand store, right? An arm here, a head there, feet from one guy, and knees from another . . ."

"You're a genetic mess," Cody observed.

Fronk opened his mouth, then got confused. Squid arms of his picked up a piece of chalk and wrote, "If you're so keen on questions, turn to page 57 in your math book, and answer the 200 questions that start there."

They all pretended to do the math problems until the bell rang. Cody spied Sully actually doing the math. Then they rose to leave for science class.

"I won't forget this outrage!" Fronk cried. "I'll catch you unawares. You'll be powerless against my mollusk strength. You'll digest slowly in my mollusk gut!"

"Whatever," Cody said. "You're too far

gone to be able to help us. Let's go."

They headed down the corridor and came upon the table with the hats again. "What are these things still doing here?" Ratface said. He reached and picked up the huge fez. "I want to try this one on."

STOP!

HEY, WHAT WAS THAT FOR? YOU COULD HAVE HAD THE NEXT TURN.

C'MON! INTO THE BOY'S BATHROOM... QUICK! I JUST REALIZED SOMETHING.

Cody set the fez down on a sink and ripped out the silk lining from the inside. "This was the hat that Mugsy put on, remember?" Cody said. "He said something in it zapped him or stung for a second or something like that. What if that was how Farley got him? This hat's so big and heavy. Maybe there's some sort of machine inside."

"But Farley told us not to wear the hats," Ratface pointed out.

"Exactly," Sully said. "He knew that's exactly what we *would* do if he told us not to."

"What a slimy trick!" Ratface cried. "That's not playing by the rules."

"Remember, it's Farley we're talking about," Sully said.

"Hey, look, guys, here it is." Sully tore off the last of the fabric. They all stared at the contraption underneath. There was a container of water with a small squid inside, a battery, a glowing rock, and a hypodermic needle.

"Unbelievable," Carlos said. "What an incredible invention!"

"You sound like you're a fan," Ratface said. "Don't forget the rotten thing this invention does."

"What's the glowing stuff?" Victor asked.

"I'm pretty sure it's radioactive material," Sully said. "Probably uranium. That must be what Professor Eelpot brought with her the night that she came. Radioactivity mutates genes. Scientists have known that for a long time."

"Speaking of science," Cody said, "we're late for science class. I don't think Professor Eelpot will overlook that."

"At least now we know about the hats," Carlos said. "We'll be on our guard. Farley won't be able to trick us so easily next time."

"Poor Mugsy, though," Ratface said, shaking his head.

CHAPTER TWELVE

THE MOVIE

They stuffed the hat parts into a bathroom stall and ran to science class, passing Dr. Farley's laboratory on the way.

"You low-down, dirty monster," Victor muttered, shaking his fist at Dr. Farley's nameplate on the door.

"C'mon. If we're late for science, she'll eat us," Cody said, tugging on Victor's arm. "Let's go."

Professor Eelpot's back was toward them as they snuck into the classroom. She was dropping a small fish into the tank belonging to Ethel, her pet electric eel.

The boys slid into their seats.

She unveiled another aquarium. The boys stared at it. They couldn't figure out what was inside. It looked like a lumpy, pointy, reddish rock.

"Is that coral?" Carlos asked.

"Behold the stonefish," Professor

Eelpot whispered. "Genus, Synanceia, species, horrida."

"Are you saying that thing's a fish?" Ratface demanded. "No way! It's too ugly. Just looks like a bumpy rock."

"Precisely," Professor Eelpot said. "That's what makes it so deadly. Class, can you all repeat the scientific name after me? Synanceia horrida."

"Sin-Nancy-a-horrible," they parroted back to her.

"The stonefish is the most venomous fish in the ocean," Professor Eelpot said. "Whereas some predators, like the mighty shark, capture their prey with their great strength and speed, the stonefish is an ambush predator. It lurks in wait at the bottom of the coral reef disguised as a rock. Lunch comes swimming by, and the stonefish chomps down on it. The stonefish's prey never suspects the stonefish isn't a rock. And if foolish humans step on the stonefish, the venom in these jagged spines can kill them." Professor Eelpot looked pleased at the thought.

"That's horrible!" Ratface gasped.

Professor Eelpot looked surprised. "No, not really," she said. "There are far too many of you humans around as it is."

"Now, class," she said, "let's watch an educational movie about ocean predators." She threaded tape from an ancient movie into an old-fashioned film projector.

"You've gotta admit, this is the best class at Splurch Academy," Carlos whispered. "She actually teaches us interesting stuff."

"Yeah," Ratface whispered. "She's a pretty good teacher. For a shark."

"Something on your minds, boys?" Professor Eelpot asked, appearing suddenly by their sides.

"No, ma'am," Cody answered.

Professor Eelpot smiled. "Exactly." She unrolled a projector screen on the front wall and dimmed the lights. Cody heard some strange mechanical sounds—something was wrong with the movie projector. Finally the film began to play. The camera showed an underwater scene with blurry fish swimming by in the distance.

"Creatures of the deep," a voice began. "Monsters so ancient, so fearsome, man still trembles at the sight of them. Hunters so deadly, no fish can stand against them."

"Fish don't stand," Carlos whispered to Cody.

"That joke is so lame, I'm embarrassed for you," Ratface whispered.

"Shh," Cody said.

"The great white shark. The anglerfish. The electric eel. The whiptailed stingray. The stonefish. The barracuda. These undersea predators are the stuff of legend. Mankind can only envy their power."

Suddenly, without warning, the movie screen snapped and rolled up into its case, and the lights switched on. Cody blinked in the brightness and did a double take. Where the screen had been, there should have been a wall and a chalkboard.

Instead . . .

"Greetings," Headmaster Farley said, standing where the screen had been, with his entire laboratory behind him. "You don't need to envy undersea creatures anymore."

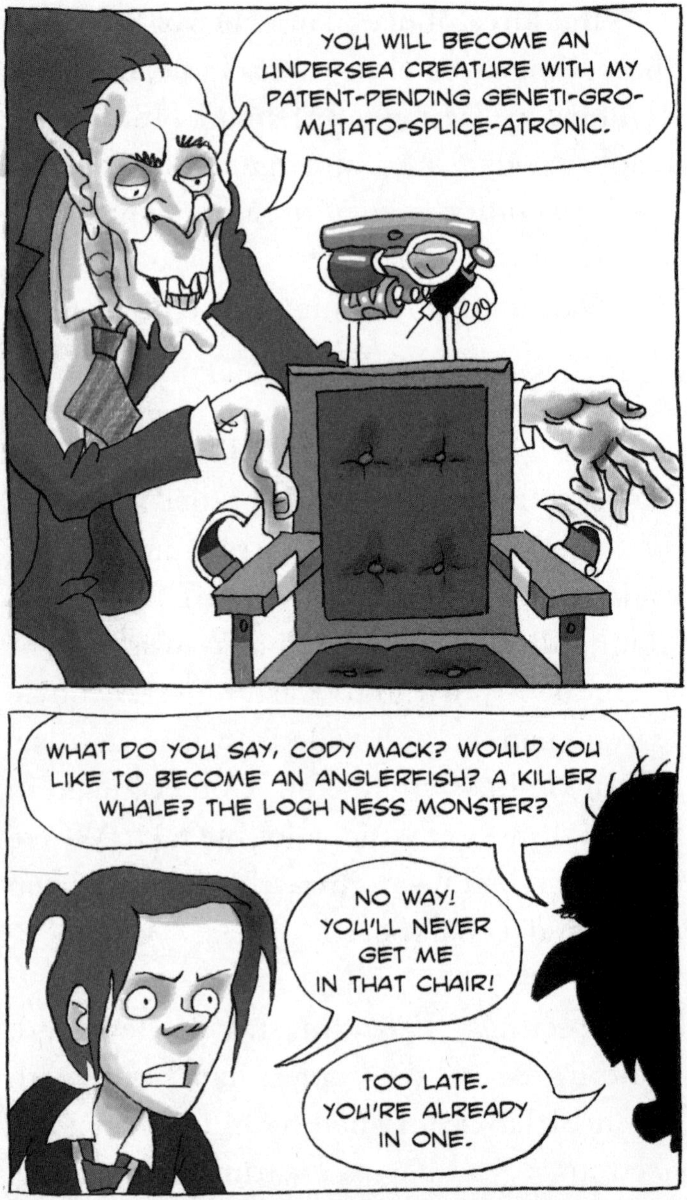
YOU WILL BECOME AN UNDERSEA CREATURE WITH MY PATENT-PENDING GENETI-GRO-MUTATO-SPLICE-ATRONIC.
WHAT DO YOU SAY, CODY MACK? WOULD YOU LIKE TO BECOME AN ANGLERFISH? A KILLER WHALE? THE LOCH NESS MONSTER?
NO WAY! YOU'LL NEVER GET ME IN THAT CHAIR!
TOO LATE. YOU'RE ALREADY IN ONE.

The boys looked up. Dangling from the ceiling over each of their heads was a Geneti-Gro-Mutato-Splice-Atronic, just like they'd found inside Mugsy's hat, loaded and pointing right at their heads.

CHAPTER THIRTEEN

THE TUBE

Eelpot walked over to Mugsy. "You can come out, Percival," she said. "No need for you to undergo the gene splicing procedure twice. Come sit on this couch with Professor Fronk."

"You're no shark," Cody yelled at Professor Eelpot. "A shark attacks with speed and power. You said so yourself. You lured us into a trap like a stupid stonefish. You're just a crummy ambush predator."

Eelpot chuckled. "You never told me, Archie, how clever your students were."

"We've got to get out of here," Carlos

hissed. "Cody! What can we do?"

Farley pressed a button, and the floor opened. Up came a widemouthed pipe with an opening like a funnel.

Professor Eelpot dipped her bucket into Ethel the electrophorus's tank and scooped her up. Then she poured Ethel into the large funnel in the laboratory floor.

Bye, Mugsy, Cody thought. *Hope I get to see you again someday. As a person, and not as a squid . . .*

"Hope he transforms in a hurry," Carlos whispered. "Either that or I hope he's a good swimmer in his human form."

"The splicing is nearly ready to begin," Farley gloated. "And then? I'll tell you what then: No more badly behaved, foul-smelling human boys requiring school lessons and cafeteria lunches! Just happy sea creatures, swimming under the sea."

"But not just sea creatures," purred Professor Eelpot. "These won't be your typical fish."

"That's right," Farley said, patting Cody on the head. "These will be sea creatures I can summon at will to do my bidding."

"I'll never do your bidding!" Cody screamed. "Get your slimy vampire hands off me!"

"Oh, but you *will* do my bidding," Farley replied. "All my monsters do my bidding. Don't they, Professor Fronk?"

The half-squid, half-corpse teacher

lolled on the sofa. It appeared that the process of turning him into a squid had progressed even further. He didn't seem to know where he was.

"Behold," Farley said, gesturing to Fronk. "Prometheus Fronk! I order you to come press the button that will activate the Geneti-Gro-Mutato-Splice-Atronic, and turn these disgusting boys into your squidly brothers!"

Fronk almost pressed the button, but his tentacled legs made him slip. While he struggled to get up again, Cody twitched in his seat. "Here we go, guys," he whispered. "Get ready to run."

"Planning an escape, Cody Mack?" Farley asked.

"You're not gonna turn me into a squid!" Cody yelled.

"Perhaps you'd prefer to be a sea sponge," Farley said with a smirk. "Then Griselda can use you to wash the dishes."

"Why don't you turn yourself into a cockroach," Cody said. "It'll feel pretty natural."

The lab door opened, and in came Miss Threadbare. "Has anyone seen Nurse Bilgewater?" she demanded. "I can't find her anywhere. She's been missing since breakfast!"

Dr. Farley coughed and looked away. Miss Threadbare got a suspicious look on her face and ripped back the curtain in the corner. There stood Nurse Bilgewater, bound and gagged.

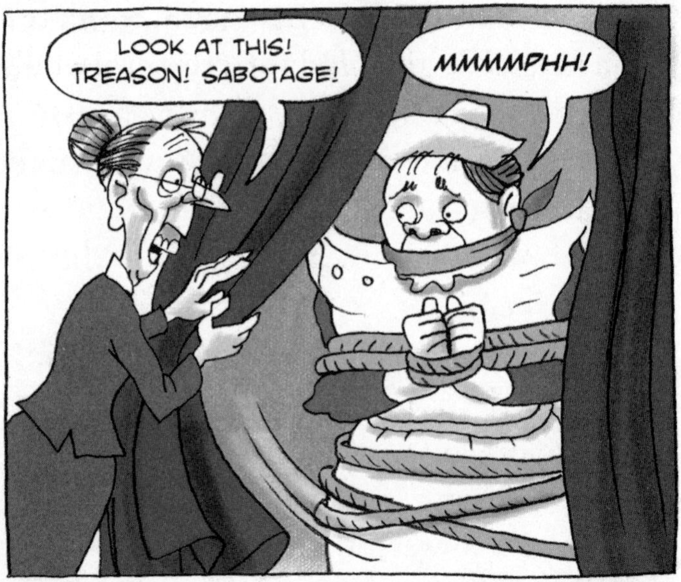
LOOK AT THIS! TREASON! SABOTAGE!
MMMMPHH!

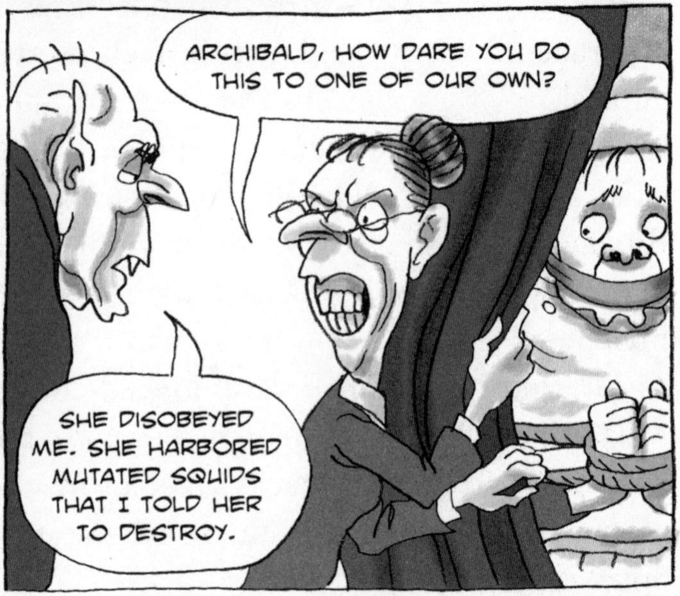
ARCHIBALD, HOW DARE YOU DO THIS TO ONE OF OUR OWN?
SHE DISOBEYED ME. SHE HARBORED MUTATED SQUIDS THAT I TOLD HER TO DESTROY.

Bilgewater spit out her gag and glared at Farley. "It's that Eelpot creature who's taken over around here," she hissed. "Archie Farley's not in charge any more. She's got him hoodwinked. That shark-face has got to go!"

"Okay, guys," Cody whispered to the others over the noise of the fighting adults. "Here's our chance. On the count of three, all of you, follow me. Don't hesitate, just go fast, okay?"

"Wait a sec," Sully said. "I've got to get something first." He ripped apart the apparatus of the Genetic-Grow-Mutato-Splice-Atronic and stuffed parts of it in his pocket.

"Quit stalling!" Victor hissed. "What are you trying to do, mutate yourself later on?"

"Trust me!" Sully whispered.

"There's only one way outta here," Cody whispered. "Down and out. Now!"

Cody bolted from his seat. The other boys followed. They charged the lab, plowing right through the teachers, and dived into the funnel.

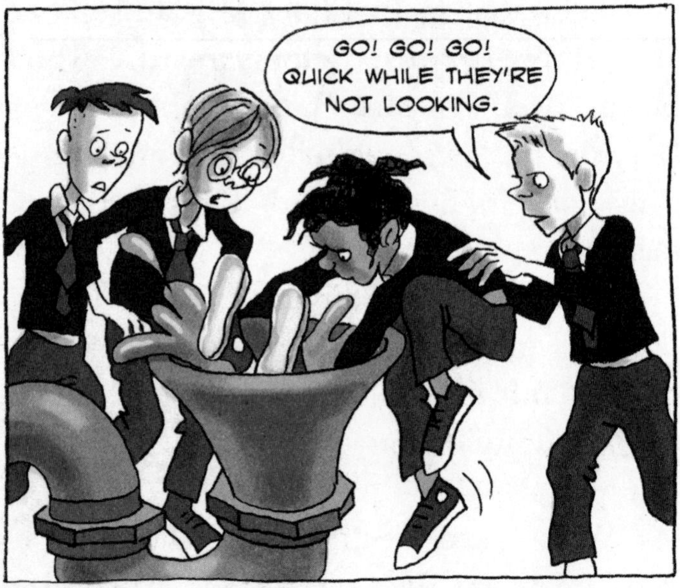
GO! GO! GO!
QUICK WHILE THEY'RE
NOT LOOKING.

CHAPTER FOURTEEN

THE SUB

They slid down the long, wet chute and landed, all five of them, on top of one another in the pool. Cody swallowed a mouthful of water. Immediately, curious, hungry squids appeared to investigate.

"They're bigger than yesterday," Ratface squawked. "Get 'em offa me!"

"Those squids are the least of your problems," Cody said. "Can everybody swim?"

They all bobbed up and down in the water, nodding. A familiar face appeared at their sides.

Cody scrambled out of the water and got into his diving suit as fast as he could. "They'll be here any second," he panted. "Our only hope is to get into the sub and get out of here."

"But how?" Carlos treaded water and flung a baby squid off his nose. "We can't all swim down that far."

"We could use that hydraulic winch if we could somehow attach the sub to it," Sully said.

"I'll swim down and attach the chain," Cody said.

Cody dived straight for the sub. Ratface

was right. The other squids were bigger now. Cody could barely see past all the squids blocking the view.

Cody clipped the chain to the submarine and swam back to the surface as fast as he could.

The winch hauled up on the chain until the sub smashed its way through the crack in the pool floor and bobbed to the surface of the water.

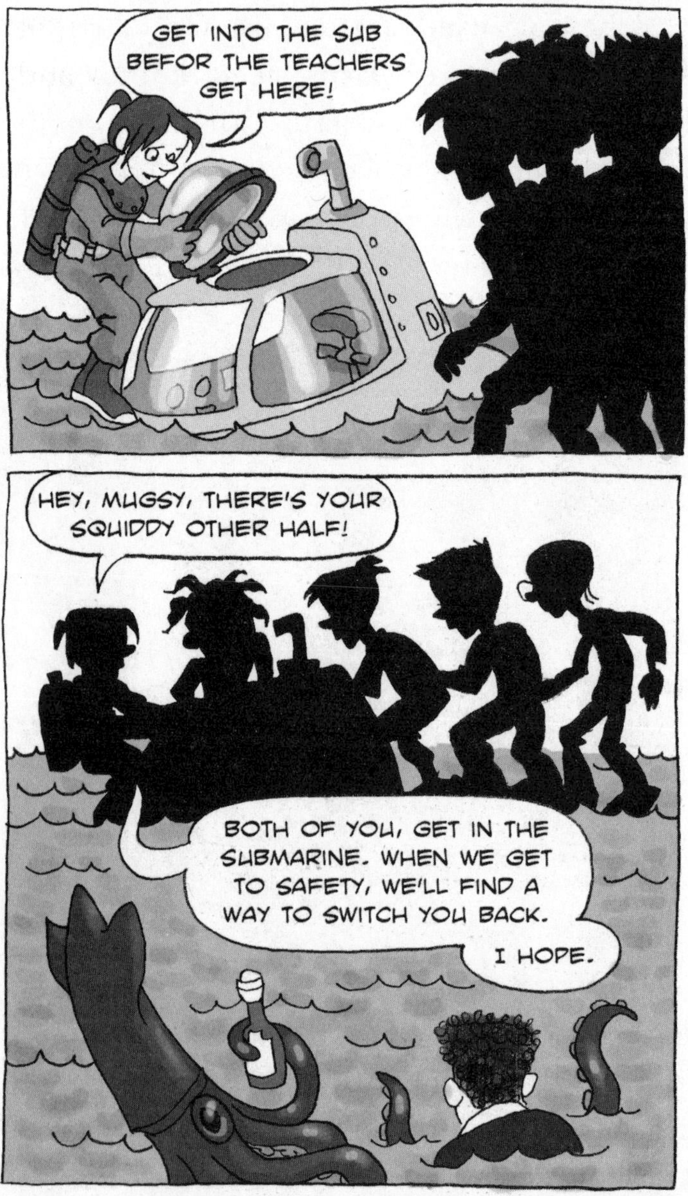
GET INTO THE SUB BEFOR THE TEACHERS GET HERE!
HEY, MUGSY, THERE'S YOUR SQUIDDY OTHER HALF!
BOTH OF YOU, GET IN THE SUBMARINE. WHEN WE GET TO SAFETY, WE'LL FIND A WAY TO SWITCH YOU BACK.
I HOPE.

They crawled inside. It was a tight squeeze in there. Arms, feet, knees, and tentacles were everywhere, with barely room left to breathe or move.

When everyone was inside the sub, Cody climbed behind the controls and tried to figure out what to do. Lights. Check. Now what?

The door to the pool room rattled. Victor and the other boys had locked it and barred it shut with oars and rescue hooks, but that only slowed the angry teachers for a moment. They smashed through the barricade. In came Farley,

Eelpot, Bilgewater, and Threadbare, still bickering loudly.

"Now would be a good time for us to disappear," Carlos told Cody. "I'm just sayin'."

Cody slammed down every lever that he could find. The submarine shuddered and groaned, then it tipped, nose-first, under the water, through the hole in the pool floor, and into the undersea cave.

"We did it!" Ratface cried. "We got away!"

"Not so fast," Sully said. "We've still got to get out of here. Preferably without drowning or causing an atomic explosion or anything. Remember, this is a nuclear-powered sub."

They sank in the dark water. Cody fumbled with the controls. "How do you drive this thing?" he muttered.

"Oh, we're dead, we're dead . . ." Ratface moaned.

Flick. Cody found the switch that turned on the lights.

"Whoa," Carlos said. "Look at that."

All around them undersea life bobbed and swayed with the gentle currents in the pool.

"Amazing," Sully said. "It's so much better than a nature show on TV."

"Hey, Cody, we're tipping to one side," Ratface said. Cody wrestled with the levers, and the sub slowly corrected itself. Cody smiled. He was catching on. They were really doing it! He was really going to drive this underwater boat out of there for good! Maybe they could get home in time for Christmas. Maybe there would be presents under the tree . . .

A speaker crackled to life on the control panel. "Cody Mack," a familiar voice cried, "this is Headmaster Farley. You get back up here at once!"

"Yeah, right," Cody shot back. "In your dreams, you lunatic bloodsucker! Adios, *non*-amigos."

The submarine lights swept along the bottom of the cave. Swimming squids swirled like butterflies on the breeze of the undersea currents in the cave.

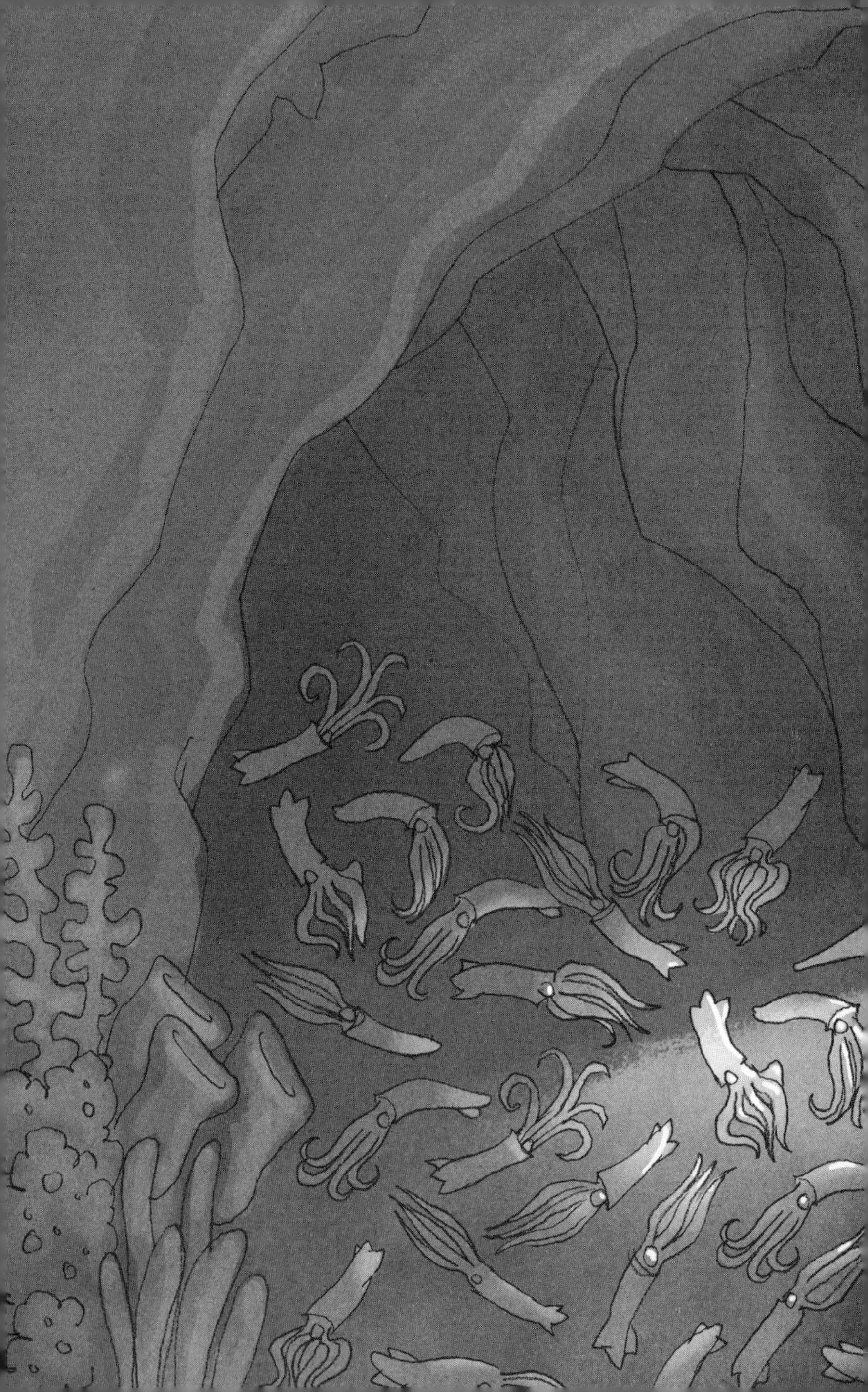

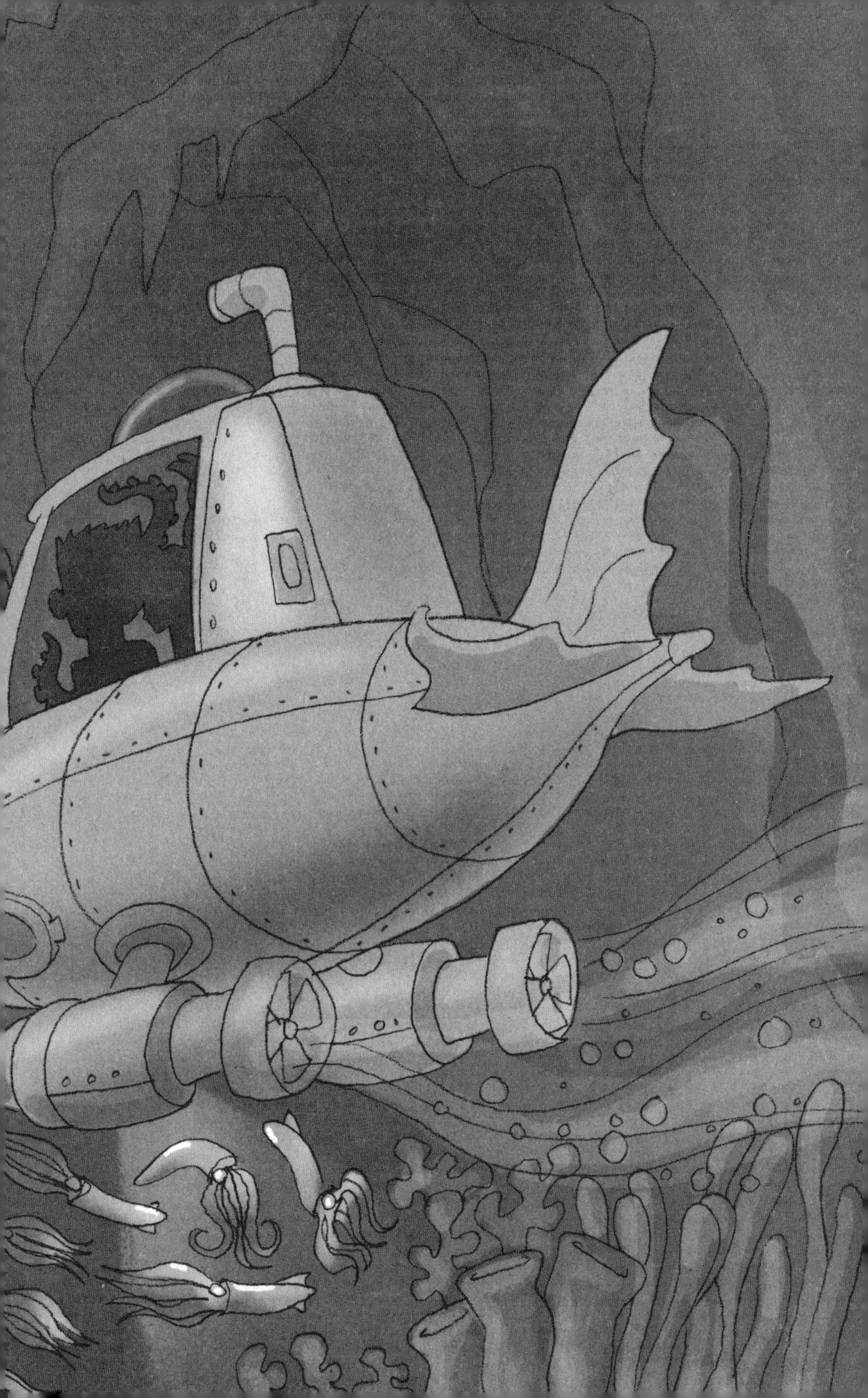

"There's got to be a way out," Cody whispered. He covered the radio with his hand so Farley wouldn't hear them. "Water gets into this cave somehow. Mugsy! Get your brother's tentacles out of my ears."

"There." Sully pointed at the cave wall.

It was a tiny crevice, barely wider than their hands.

"That must be why all the squids are trapped in here," Carlos said.

"So we're stuck," Ratface said. "Our big getaway is doomed!"

SOMETHING SLAMMED SO HARD INTO THE SIDE OF THE SUB THAT IT MADE A DENT.

Something slammed into the other side.

"Hello, boys," Farley's voice called through the radio. "That's Professor Eelpot in her true shape, knocking on your door. I don't suppose you'd like her to succeed in tearing your sub apart, would you? Remember that since you left the pool you are no longer on the grounds of Splurch Academy. When Dr. Eelpot reaches you, her only difficulty will be choosing which boy to eat first."

"Then let's not let her reach us," Cody said. "Weapons ready?"

"Check," Sully said.

FIRE TORPEDO!

WWHOOSHH!

THOOM-THOOM-THOOM. A cloud of murky dust erupted up ahead. When the water settled, they saw that the torpedo had opened a wider hole in the cave wall. Tiny squids began escaping through the hole, while little fish began streaming inside.

WHAM! Professor Eelpot punched the nose of the submarine so viciously a pane of glass cracked.

"We won't survive this," Sully wailed. "The ship can't take it much longer!"

"He's ri-ight," Farley's voice crackled.

"Zip your dead lips, Farley," Cody shouted. "FIRE TORPEDO." Victor punched a button. The other torpedo came spiraling out of its case and racing toward Eelpot. Once again, she avoided it.

THOOM-THOOM-SHEBOOM. The fissure in the cave wall opened even wider.

Professor Eelpot, the human shark, swam into view once more in front of the sub. She wiggled her fearsome sharky body like she was having tons of fun playing a game of chase. Then she bolted forward, her jaws stretched wide.

Cody let go of the controls. This was it. There were no more torpedoes.

"Bye, guys," he whispered.

CHAPTER FIFTEEN

THE TORPEDO

FWWWUMP!

Something knocked Eelpot off course—
something so heavy and so fast and furious
it was like an underwater charging bull.

"It's Bilgewater!" Ratface cried, peering
through the sub windows at the creature
brawling with Eelpot. "See her nurse's cap?
Bilgewater saved us!"

"She *what*?" Farley screeched in the
radio. "Tell her to stop! This will be noted
on her yearly performance evaluation."

"Stuff a squid in it, Farley," Cody yelled.
"We're gone!"

Eelpot and Bilgewater went tumbling, tail over tentacle, in an epic battle, leaving a clear path for the sub to exit the cave and sail underwater all the way to New York City or Chesapeake or, for that matter, Singapore.

"See you later, Splurch," Cody sang, punching the levers forward. "Here we go!" He focused on the controls and steering the sub carefully through the still-narrow opening in the cave wall.

"What was that?" Carlos said.

"What?" Cody muttered.

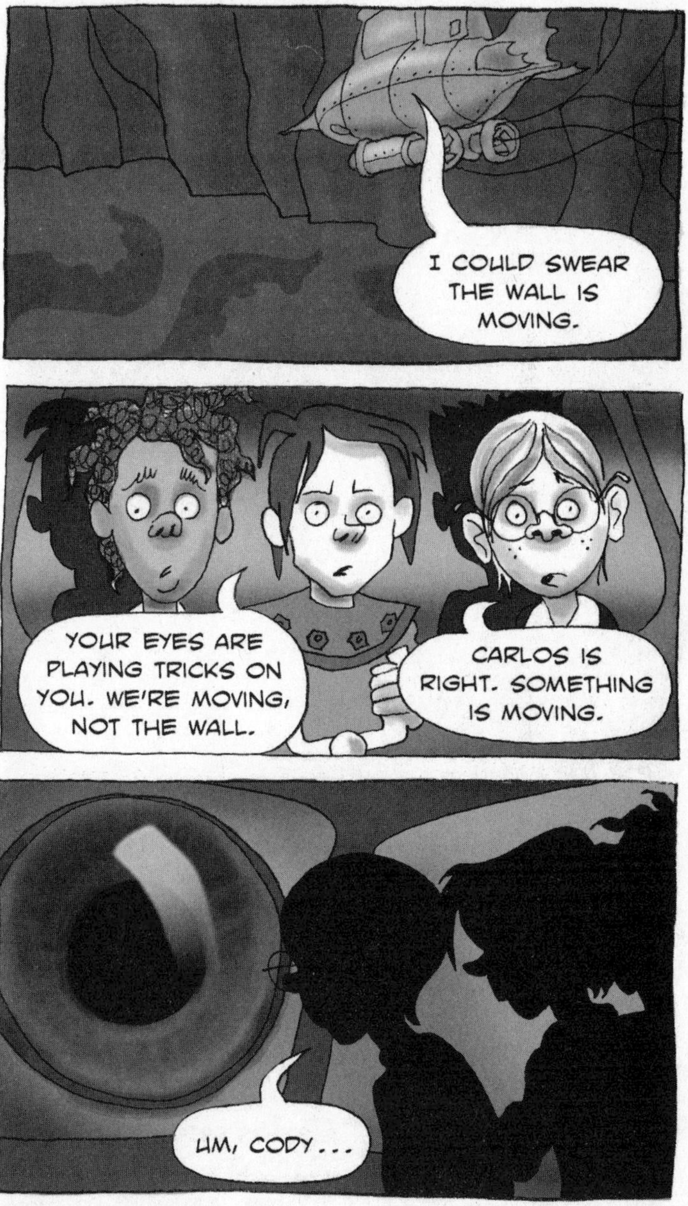
I COULD SWEAR THE WALL IS MOVING.
YOUR EYES ARE PLAYING TRICKS ON YOU. WE'RE MOVING, NOT THE WALL.
CARLOS IS RIGHT. SOMETHING IS MOVING.
UM, CODY...

It was a squid so massive, its trunk was like a redwood tree, its arms like elephant trunks, and its suckers like toilet plungers. It was the hugest living creature Cody had ever laid eyes on. But what chilled Cody's blood in his veins was the squid's face—if you can call it that on a squid. As Cody got close enough to see it, he saw that all around its skin were scars, running in long, jaggedy lines all over its exposed surface. Whereas all the other squids ranged

from white to pink to red in color, this big monster was a sickly grayish-green.

"That's no squid," Sully breathed. "That's a Frankensquid."

"What?" Victor said, incredulous. "How? Why?"

Sully pointed behind them to Mugsy and his squiddy twin. "This squid was mutated with Mugsy's DNA. That one"—he pointed to the massive monster squid outside—"was mutated with Fronk's."

"Try to maneuver around it and get out through the hole," Ratface said. "Fast!"

"Give me maximum power, Victor," Cody said. "Squeeze all you can get out of that nuclear reactor."

They accelerated toward the opening. The mighty squid sailed by. Had it noticed the submarine? Maybe not! Could they scooch on by him through the gap in the wall and onto freedom?

"Almost there," Ratface chanted. "Almost clear! No squiddy corpse monster's gonna keep *me* from getting home!"

The nose of the sub was through the crack . . . its headlights were sweeping a broad expanse of ocean floor . . .

SNAP.

Their heads jerked forward and then their necks snapped back.

"We're stuck!" Ratface cried. "We need more power to break through!"

Sully shook his head. "We're not stuck on the rocks," he said. "We're caught."

Long, tentacled arms wrapped themselves around the sub's windows and sides. It pulled the underwater boat back inside the cave, overpowering the nuclear reactor engine like it was run by hamsters. The massive Frankensquid had their submarine in its clutches. It flung the submarine against the back of the cave, sending it skidding across the sand and crashing into the shipwreck. Then it advanced on them again. They saw its full bulk approaching them, slow and green and menacing in the boat's headlights.

Cody struggled to steer the submarine out of the tangled wreckage.

For the first time since he had transformed, Mugsy spoke.

165

Mugsy knocked his head against the buttons Victor had used to fire at Eelpot. "Us!"

"I think he wants you to shoot him and his squid brother out like torpedoes," Sully said. Mugsy nodded hard. "Yeah, that's right, that's what he wants."

"He'll eat you guys like lollipops," Cody protested. "Guys, talk him out of it!"

But Mugsy and his squid brother grew more insistent. Finally Cody nodded. They slithered into the weapons canisters, lickety-split.

The giant squid was nearly upon them now. Cody aimed the sub straight at it.

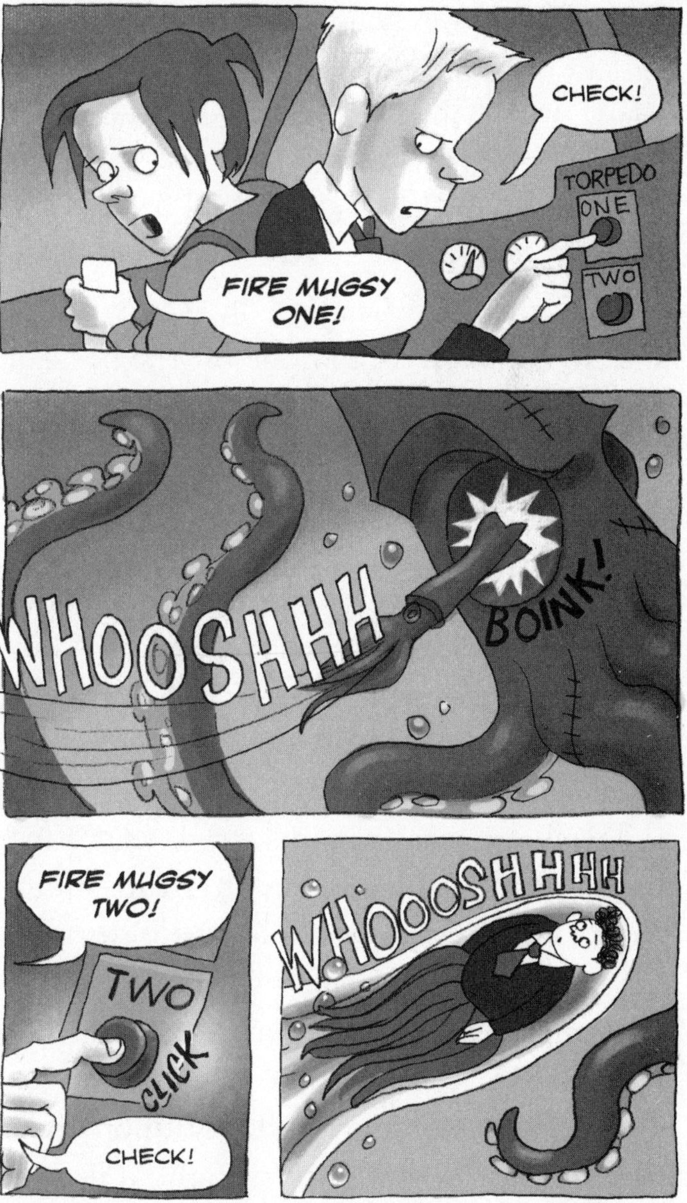
FIRE MUGSY ONE!
CHECK!
TORPEDO
ONE
TWO
WHOOSHHH
BOINK!
FIRE MUGSY TWO!
TWO
CLICK
CHECK!
WHOOOSHHHH

"What's going on down there?" Farley demanded over the radio. "What do you mean, 'Fire Mugsy Two'? Get up here this instant."

"Are they okay?" Cody said. "Can you see? Can you tell?"

Sully shook his head. "Can't see a thing," he said. "We'll have to hope for the best for them."

"So much for that," Victor said. "Got anything else we can shoot?"

"Here's Mugsy's ketchup bottle," Carlos said. "Maybe we can use it to send our parents a message. A final good-bye." Cody maneuvered the sub for one last desperate shot at the breech in the cave wall.

SCHLOOMP.

Two long, massive arms wrapped around the sub and pulled it toward the squid. Their view disappeared in a sea of churning legs. The lights of the sub illuminated a chomping beak and a gaping mouth.

GULP.

The Frankensquid swallowed the sub.

CHAPTER SIXTEEN

THE BUTTON

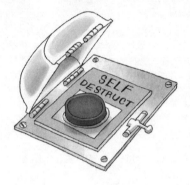

All they could see were squid innards everywhere they looked. Everything was strangely calm and quiet. The lights of the sub illuminated the grayish inner body walls of the massive squid. The engine sloshed in the squid's vat of stomach acid. Even inside the great creature there were surgical stitch marks!

"Geez, he's a Frankensquid, inside and out," Ratface said.

Sully whipped a pencil and notebook from his pocket and began to sketch. "This is amazing."

"Does this squid count as living if it's part Fronk?" Carlos asked. "Isn't it more of an undead zombie squid?"

"I can't believe you guys are debating this." Victor ran a hand through his hair. "We're all going to DIE, and nobody will ever see Sully's eyewitness drawings, and no one will care whether the Frankensquid is living. It'll be a lot more living than we will be in another few minutes."

"Good thing Mugsy and Mugsy got out when they did," Carlos said. "Now maybe they can be free together. Squid brothers for life. At least someone will remember us, maybe, after we're gone."

"What's it gonna feel like to be digested?" Ratface's voice quivered. "Slow and painful?"

"We're not dead yet," Cody told him, flipping every lever and pressing every button he could find. "So long as we're alive, we fight! Let's give this Frankensquid a monster stomachache."

From inside his dark body, they heard the Frankensquid groan and gurgle. They heard the thump of its heart and the shooshing of its blood through its veins. Every sound the hideous creature made was amplified inside. Every move it made made their stomachs slosh.

Dr. Farley's voice fizzed over the radio once more. "Boys! Are you still down there? I request a status report immediately."

"Our status is mind your beeswax, Farley, and leave us alone." Cody covered the radio again and addressed the other boys. "Guys, help me," he said. "I've pressed every button. I don't know what else to do. Look for anything I may have missed. Some hidden switch? Something?"

"Here's one that says 'Release stale air,'" Victor said. "That oughtta give our Frankensquid a major stomachache."

"And a case of the burps," Cody said. "Let's do it." He jammed his finger on the button.

Huge bubbles of air exited the sub. "Hope it leaves enough for us," Sully said.

The monster squid made a grunting sound that echoed through the boys' ears.

Then it squeezed its body together so tightly that more panes of window glass cracked on the sub. Squid stomach juices began pouring into the sub.

"We're gonna drown!" Ratface yelled. "Our pitiful lives will end desolving in squid digestive acid!"

Farley's voice crackled over the speakers once more, issuing orders to his staff members beside the pool. "Prometheus Fronk," he said in a deep voice. "You are my monster servant now. I command you to go get those boys and bring them to me."

From over the radio, they heard a loud *SPLASH*.

"That's Fronk, jumping in to try and find us," Cody said. "Lotsa luck, Fronkie. You'll never be able to beat this huge guy."

Suddenly the giant Frankensquid's movements stopped.

"Bring the boys to me," Dr. Farley repeated. "Bring them to me now."

The Frankensquid started to swim off again. They could feel the pulsations of its body.

From deep inside the squid, Cody heard deep, groaning sounds. "Aaaaaaaarr . . . Eeeeeeeee . . . Mmmmmaaasssss . . . Errrrrrrrrrrr . . ."

"The squid is talking!" Sully cried.

"No way," Ratface said. "Maybe it's trying to go to the bathroom. Don't you ever talk to yourself in the bathroom? Sometimes I sing."

And then it all clicked in Cody's head. *Talk to yourself* . . . Fronk, the teacher, jumping in the water, and the giant Frankensquid, grunting and swimming. He covered the microphone so Farley couldn't hear the squid's sounds. Aarr . . . Eeee . . . Mmaasss . . . Errr . . . *Farley, Master!*

"Guys," he said. "The Frankensquid's not fighting with Fronk. The Frankensquid IS Fronk. He's become Farley's slave somehow, and he's bringing us back to his master."

"We are so doomed," Ratface said. "Doomder than doomed."

Cody's mind raced.

"I hope Mugsy has a happy life," Ratface sniffed. He wiped his eyes. "I hope he finds himself a nice squid girl someday, and they have little squid babies, and maybe they could name them after us."

"Disgusting!" Carlos said. "A squid wife? And babies? Gross!"

"Quit the sappy stuff," Victor said.

The other boys nodded. They all stared at one another. It was the end, and they knew it. Nobody could speak. Nobody needed to. Then Victor noticed a button.

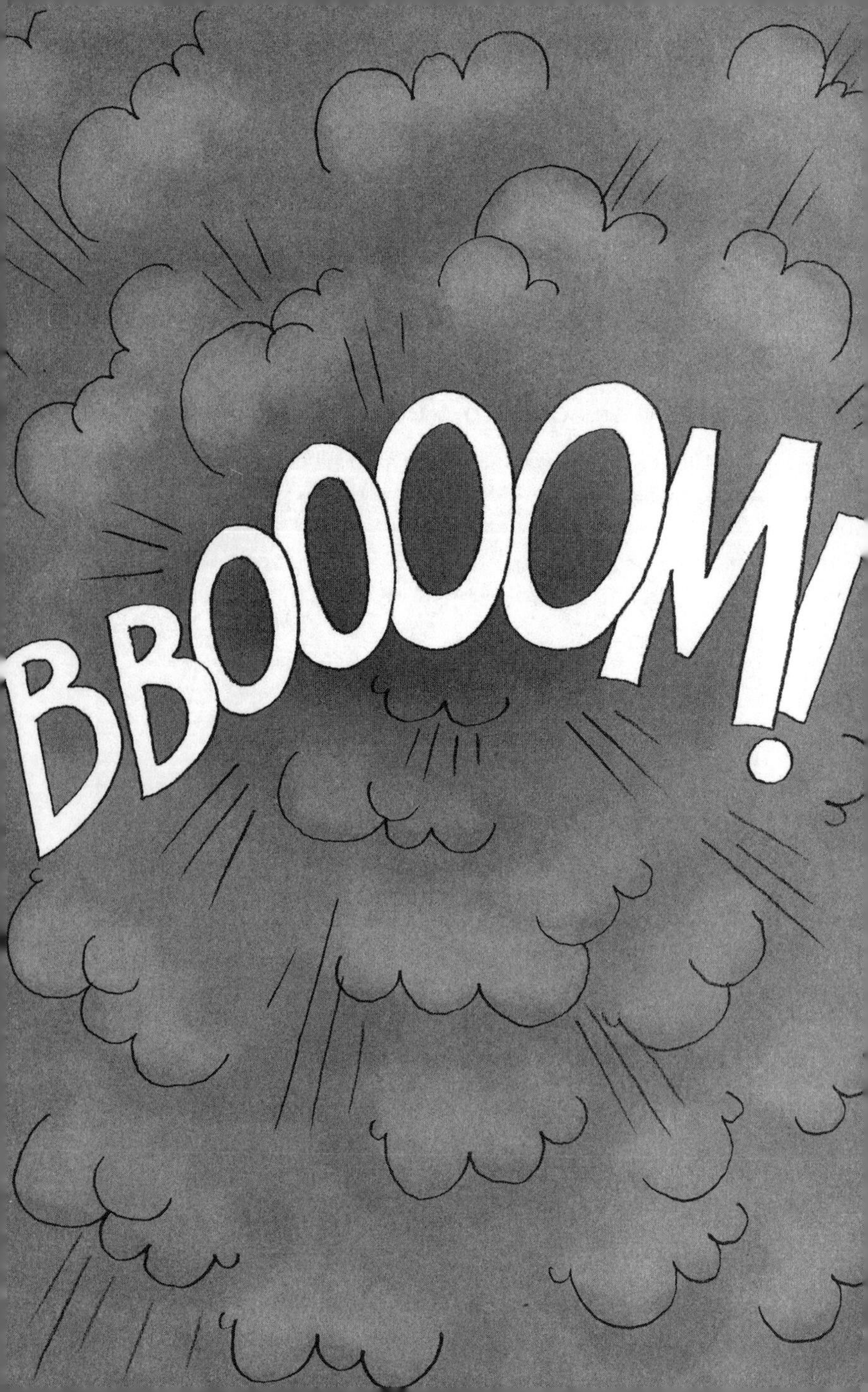
BBOOOOM!!

CHAPTER SEVENTEEN

THE EEL

Everything went black.

Everything went white.

Everything went helter-skelter, spinning like a tornado, roaring like the end of the world, sizzling like bacon fat in a frying pan. Arcs of high-voltage electricity snaked out from the exploding ship. Clouds of atomic radiation blossomed like ashy flowers. And chunks of foul, putrid, gray-green, undead squid flesh rained down on the whole world, slapping the pool like hailstones, slapping the spectators like rotten fish burgers from above.

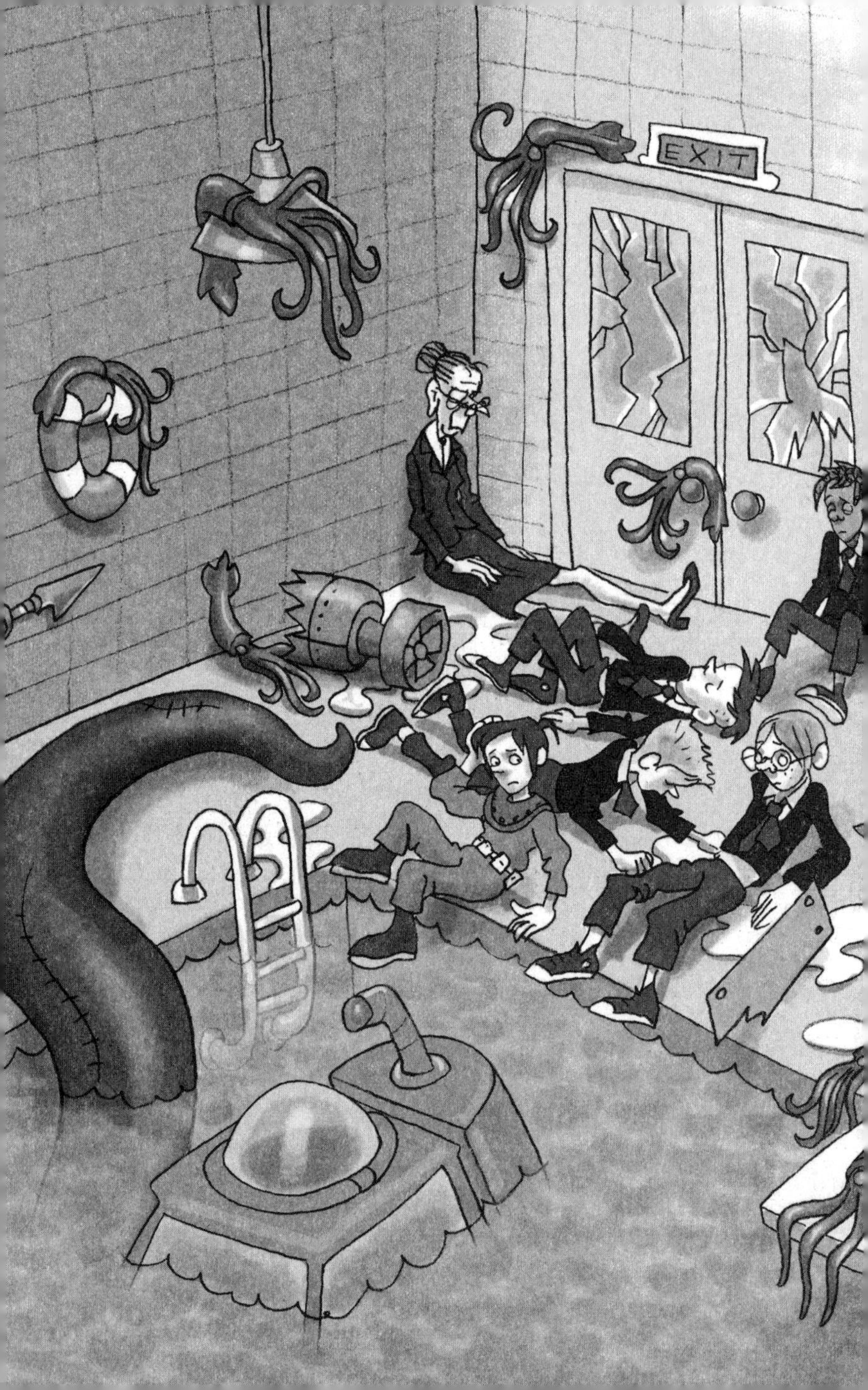
EXIT

Cody opened his eyes and saw nothing but light. *Am I in heaven?* he wondered. He shook himself. *What would the odds of that be? We survived. I can't believe it.*

On the deck of the pool, buried under a huge Franken-tentacle, lay Dr. Farley, temporarily stunned and unconscious. *Good*, Cody thought. *He can stay that way.* Not far off, lying facedown, was Mr. Fronk—with his own legs back. *Hey, he got unsquidified*, Cody thought.

Miss Threadbare clambered to her feet and watched the water anxiously. "Bilgey?" she called. "Bilgey, are you all right?"

But there was no sign of the octopus nurse. Miss Threadbare paced, growing more anxious each second.

Then Nurse Bilgewater's body rose, bobbing to the surface, facedown. Miss Threadbare shrieked in dismay, then fished her from the water with a rescue hook.

Bilgewater sat there in a soggy heap while Threadbare fanned the air in front of her face.

Cody looked over at Carlos and Sully, who'd crawled over beside him. "Explain?"

Sully adjusted his glasses. "Who can explain anything around here?"

"Well, for starters, how is Professor Fronk back to normal?" Cody asked.

"Ah." Sully scratched his head. "I guess the radiation from the nuclear fallout reversed the spliced mutations. Remember how Farley had to use radioactive rocks to mutate and transfer the genes in the first place? This time Fronk got his genes back from the Frankensquid. Probably the Frankensquid got his genes back from Fronk before he blew up."

"I'm not sorry to see that big, gross squid gone," Ratface said. "Eating us? Not cool. And those stitches inside his belly gave me the creeps."

Carlos wiped his nose on his sleeve. "Too bad Mugsy and his twin squid couldn't get fixed, too," he said. "Poor Mugsy."

Cody hung his head. "I doubt Mugsy and his brother survived their encounter with the Frankensquid."

"It's a miracle that we did," Sully said. He turned away.

Cody felt something tickle his ear. Another pesky squid! Without thinking, he slapped the curious tentacle away.

"Don't do that," Carlos cried. "It's Mugsy!"

"It's both of them!" Ratface squeaked. "They're alive!"

Nurse Bilgewater woke from her stupor and pointed a shaky finger at the Mugsys. "It was them," she told Miss Threadbare.

Sully pulled something off the apparatus he'd been carrying around and tossed it to where the Mugsy squids still bobbed and thrashed in the water.

"What's Sully doing?" Ratface asked.

Cody thought hard. "Trying to bring Mugsy back," he said. "It's radioactive rock. Radiation reversed Fronk's procedure. It's our only chance for Mugsy. Maybe it'll transform them back."

But the radioactive rocks didn't help Mugsy at all. He and his squid brother still bobbed together in the water, with happy, vacant, small-brained expressions on their faces.

"What else do we need?" Victor asked. "It's not fair that that lug nut Fronk gets back to normal and not our Mugs!"

Sully shook his head. For once, apparently, his big brain wasn't big enough to fix things. Dr. Farley, who looked like he'd been hit by a truck, crawled to the edge of the pool. Just then a shark heaved itself out of the water and tried to slide onto the deck, but somehow it seemed too exhausted. The creature transformed itself back into Professor Eelpot.

She looked like she'd seen better days. In fact, she seemed like she could barely swim. She reached for something dangling over the edge of the pool—Farley's hand, in fact. She gave it a tug, but instead of using it to help her out of the water, she pulled the headmaster in.

Cody and the boys burst out laughing.

"Serves them right," Cody said.

"Should we help them?" Carlos whispered to Cody.

"No way," Cody said. "Farley looks nastier than ever when he's wet."

"I wouldn't have thought it was possible," Ratface said.

Professor Eelpot bobbed to the surface, stuck her fingers between her teeth, and blew a feeble whistle.

As if in answer, something long and gray streaked toward the water, straight to Professor Eelpot.

"It's Ethel!" Carlos cried, pointing to the electric eel.

It wriggled like a shot back to its master, passing in between the two Mugsys on its way to Professor Eelpot and Dr. Farley.

"Watch out, Mugsy!" Cody cried. "She'll zap you!"

And sure enough, Ethel did zap them. A jolt of electricity fizzed between the squid brothers. Their squiddy eyes rolled back in their heads, and they both sank to the bottom of the pool.

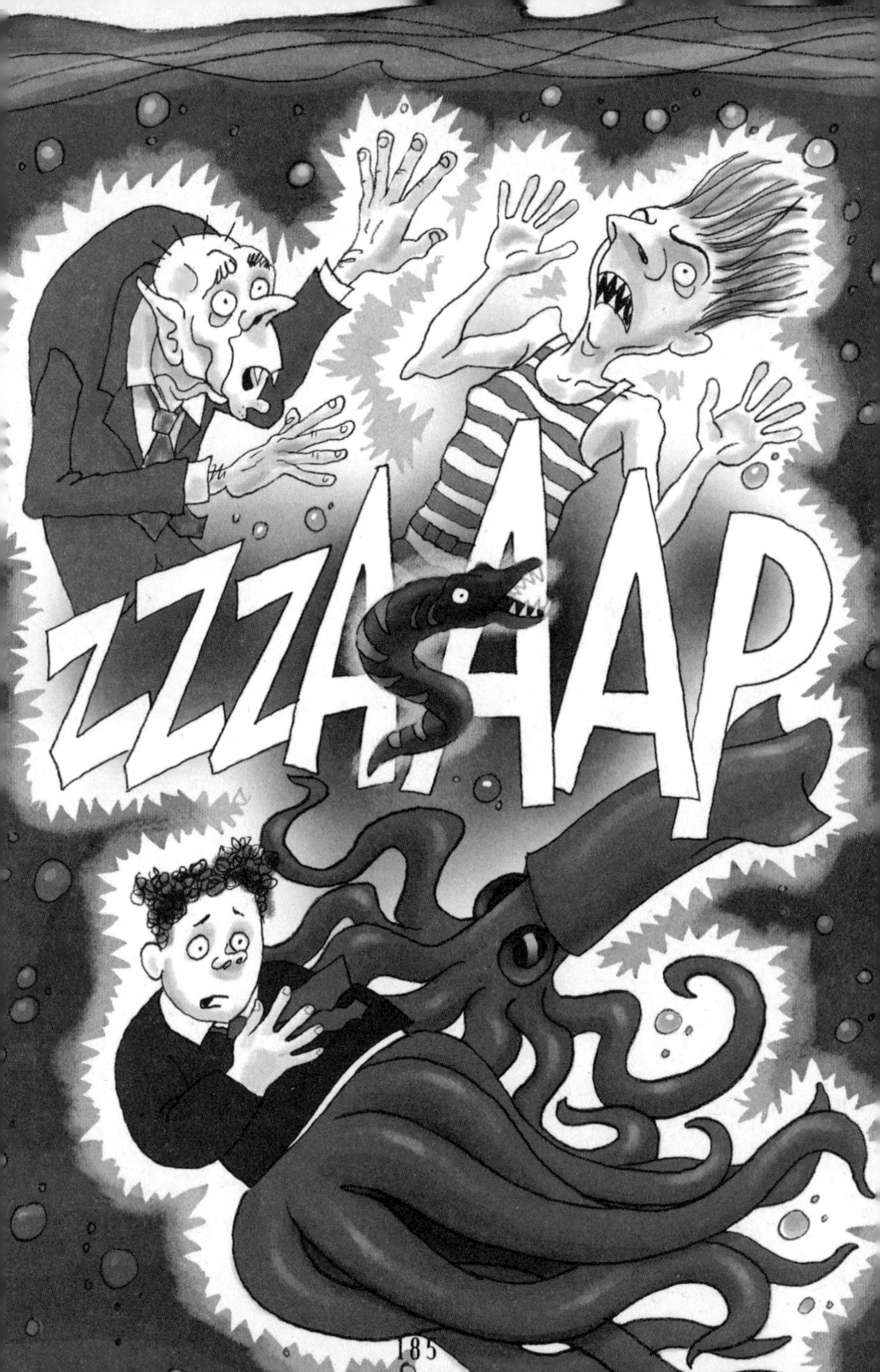
ZZZAAAP

"Help them!" Ratface cried. "They've been stunned! They'll drown!"

Smoke rose from Farley's and Eelpot's wet hair. Mugsy and his brother weren't the only ones stunned.

Cody staggered to his feet, getting ready to dive in to save Mugsy, but before he could, Mugsy's wet, curly head broke the surface of the pool. He swam easily to the ladder and climbed out.

Not the least bit squiddy.

Mugsy sank onto a pile of life jackets and closed his eyes like a baby ready for a nap.

"He saved *us*," Cody said. "Mugsy's the real hero. Both of him!"

"Electricity!" Carlos said. "That's what the mutation needed. A jump start! That's how it worked for Fronk. All that electricity and radiation from the exploding sub. It makes perfect sense!"

"Riiiight," Victor said, rolling his eyes. "*Perfect* sense."

"Yeah," Sully said. "The uranium would create the mutation, but you'd still need electricity to accelerate the transformation. Radioactivity plus electricity. It makes perfect sense. Of course!"

Mugsy opened his eyes. "What happened?" he said. "Where am I? I . . . I dreamed there were two of me. And that I liked to eat fish." He searched the surface of the pool. "*Was* it a dream? Where's the other me?"

"Heading off to sea, I think," Cody said, watching the water. "Like happy squids do. Adios, Other Mugsy."

LOOKS LIKE EELPOTTY AND FARLEY'VE HAD THEIR BRAINS A WEE BIT SCRAMBLED.

"Ooh, did they mutate with each other?" Nurse Bilgewater, who seemed to be feeling much better, rose to her feet and reached out a hook to grab the soggy villains. "Wouldn't that be a lovely combination. We could call them both 'Sharkula.' Or 'VampFish.' Or 'The Great White Undead.'"

"No such luck, Beulah," Threadbare said. "They both seem to be themselves. But they look like they're going to need long-term medical care to restore them to normal."

Nurse Bilgewater rubbed her hands together. Just for fun, she flicked Farley's nose. He didn't even flinch. She giggled. "Why should we restore them to normal?" she said happily. "Normal for them wasn't so hot. I could also make a few surgical improvements."

"Whatever you think is best." Miss Threadbare patted her on the shoulder. "They're your patients now. Come on. Let's get them to the infirmary." Together they dragged Farley and Eelpot away, none too gently.

"How long do you think Farley will have mush for brains?" Ratface asked.

"Probably not long enough," Cody said. "Maybe long enough for us to find a way to escape."

"I've been thinking," Carlos said. "It wouldn't be hard to rig a telephone wire from the roof . . ."

"So, what'd I miss, guys?" Mugsy said. "I'm starving. Is there anything good to eat? I feel like I haven't had ketchup in a thousand years."

Cody and the other boys hoisted Mugsy up on their shoulders and carried him out of the pool room, hero-style. It wasn't easy to do.

"Welcome home, Mugs," Cody said. "It's great to have you back. Let's go steal you some ketchup. And a whole box of doughnuts to go with it."

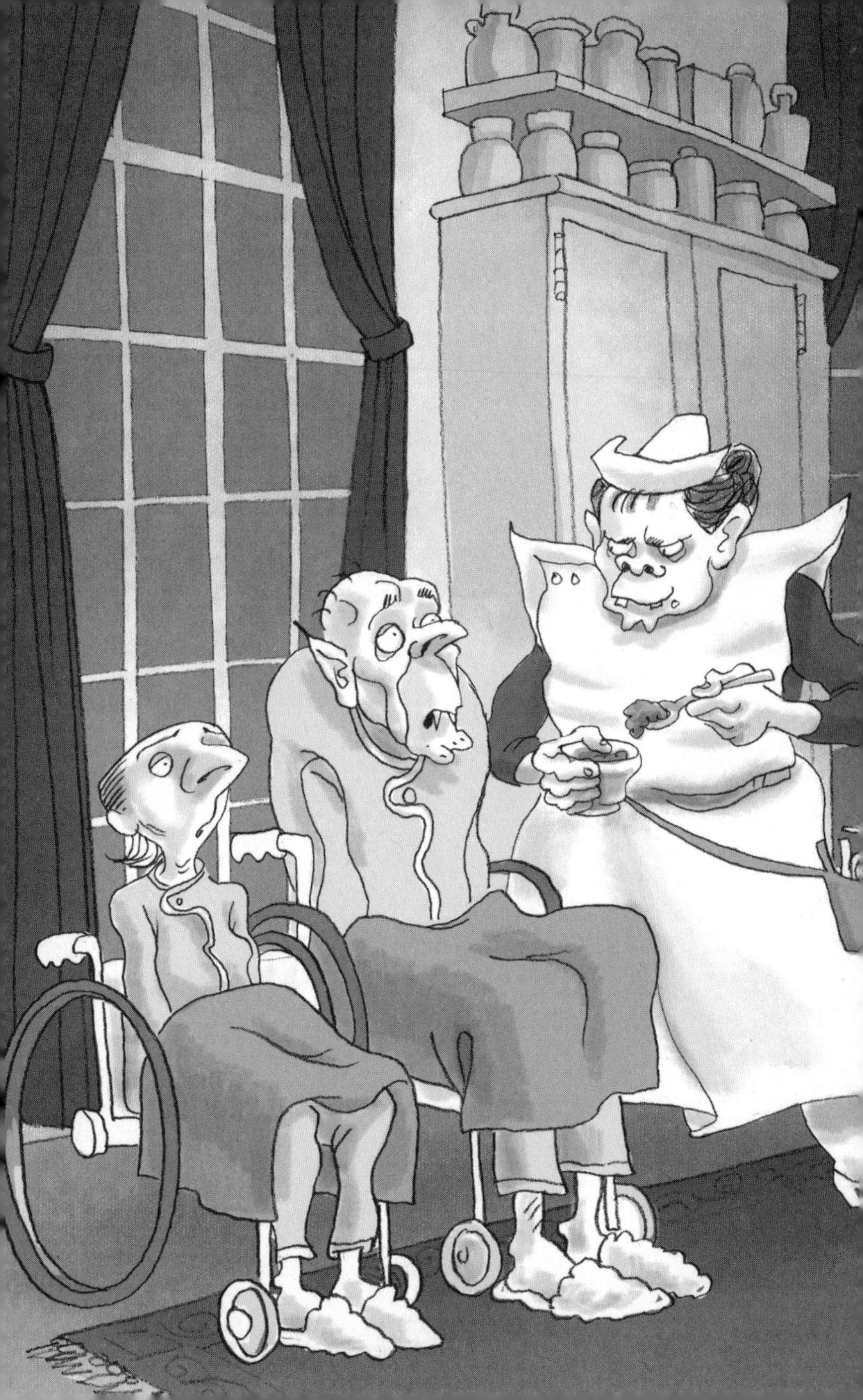

Acknowledgments

Special thanks to our sister Beth,
without whom Eelpot might
not smell as sweet.

About the Authors

Sally Faye Gardner and Julie Gardner Berry are sisters, both originally from upstate New York. Sally, who now lives in New York City with a smallish black dog named Dottie, has, at various times, worked as a gas pumper, janitor, sign painter, meeting attendee, and e-mail sender. Julie, who now lives near Boston with her husband, four smallish sons, and tiger cat named Coco, has worked as a restaurant busboy, volleyball referee, cleaning lady, and seller of tight leather pants. Today she, too, attends meetings and sends e-mail. Julie is the author of *The Amaranth Enchantment* and *Secondhand Charm*, while this is Sally's first series.